The

Mute of Anthony College
and the
Three Professors

A Victorian Mystery

by

Alydia Rackham

THE THREE PROFESSORS

Copyright © 2020 Alydia Rackham

All rights reserved.

ISBN: 9798637180431

Special thanks to these Patreon patrons:
Karen, Kathryn, Jon and Noel

Chapter One

Friday, December 15th

1882

"For heaven's sake, Basil—how long has this teacup *been* here?" Imogen cried, lifting the stained white cup into the air and raising her eyebrows indignantly at her brother. "The tea has *dried* inside of it—the porcelain has turned positively black."

"That isn't tea," Basil rumbled in reply, standing in his stocking feet on a stepstool near the staircase bookshelf. "It's ink."

"Ink! In a teacup?" Imogen cried, making a face down into it. "You're a savage."

"I'm not going to be blamed for that," Basil replied, climbing nimbly up on top of the bookshelf and stretching his legs out on its length. *"Someone* broke my inkwell."

Victoria Thulin suppressed a smile as she lifted a stack of books off a side table, listening with amusement as brother and sister bickered back and forth. The three of them occupied Pendywick Place's front parlor library, a large, backward-L-shaped room lined with shelves and stacked with miscellaneous books, writing utensils, papers, tea things, a typewriter on the crowded desk, and a lamp standing in every single place it was possible to set a lamp.

The grand piano was laden with dozens and dozens more books that hadn't found homes on the shelves. The room smelled of books, of course, and of firewood. Mrs. Imogen Fleetwood, her beautiful blonde hair done up in a simple bun, and wearing a white blouse and stylish blue skirt, bustled around the parlor, arms full of books and papers, striving to put each in its proper place—or to *find* a place for everything that clearly had never been put away. Victoria, her own black hair done back and out of the way, and wearing a dark red dress she'd been accustomed to lately, had been enlisted to help her soon-to-be-sister-in-law in the monumental task of making the parlor ready for Christmas.

Basil Collingwood, Victoria's tall, distinguished fiancé, had been no help at all so far. Instead, he had donned his velvet dressing gown over his shirt, waistcoat and trousers, elected to take up a book and mount his customary shelf to read. As Victoria glanced up at him, she remembered with vivid clarity the very first time she had seen him at Pendywick Place: sitting just there, wearing grey trousers and waistcoat, his sleeves rolled up, his spectacles catching the glint of the lamp, his short, curly dark hair falling across his forehead...

His lightning-grey eyes finding her, his dark brow furrowing, his long, elegant hands wrapped around a massive volume of Milton...

He had seemed so forbidding then—even terrifying. But now, as he teased about the inkwell—the inkwell *Victoria* had broken last year in her utter frustration, before she had learned sign language—she met his sideways glance. And he smiled secretively at her. That genuine smile that touched the edges of his eyes with warm, merry lines. She grinned back—and winked at him.

He chuckled.

"I cannot for the life of me understand how you could ever find anything in this place," Imogen muttered, having missed their exchange. She scanned the bindings of the books on the shelves.

"I only have trouble when my elder sister thinks she needs to rearrange," Basil retorted, flipping the book open.

"Nonsense," Imogen answered back, finding the correct place, alphabetically, for the book she held—and then beginning to shove the other books to make a space. "You simply can't—ugh!—*entertain* with the place looking like this!"

"Entertain?" Basil twisted and gave her a look. "Who the devil am I going to be entertaining?"

Imogen rammed the book into the tiny space she had created, then turned and faced him with a huff.

"You aren't the only one living here anymore," she reminded him. "This is Father and Mother's house, and soon it will be Victoria's too. And James and I will be here constantly." She put a hand on her hip. "Do you expect us all to live like misanthropic bachelors? Make Pendywick Place another chapter of your Diogenes Club?"

"Not a bad idea at all," Basil muttered, turning a page. "A little peace and quiet—"

"Well, there's been far too much of that here these past years," Imogen countered, ramming another book into place. "Although I understand you *did* make Christmas here last year?" Imogen looked at Victoria, who had drawn up beside her.

Since her arms were full, Victoria couldn't elaborate, but she did nod. Imogen leaned closer to her, her bright eyes sparkling.

"You have no idea how jealous I was of all of you when I got Basil's letter. I haven't had a proper Christmas since I was a girl. Where did you say you put the tree?"

Victoria set the books down on the piano, and pointed to a space directly across from the fireplace.

"And you had garlands?" Imogen pressed.

/ *Yes, on the bannisters,*/ Victoria signed.

"And Christmas dinner? With pudding?" Imogen said, her eyebrows drawing together in longing.

/ *Of course,*/ Victoria grinned. / *What would Christmas be without pudding?*/

"Oh, Basil!" Imogen sighed keenly, sending a wistful look to her brother. "I simply can't wait—it's almost painful. I feel like a ridiculous child."

"I don't know what else is new," Basil muttered into his book.

Imogen's eyes narrowed to slits, she took up a pencil, and threw it like a knife straight at her brother. It twirled through the air like a deadly dart and *thwacked* him right in the side of the arm.

"Ow!" Basil cried, twitching around in surprise—

Victoria burst out laughing. Imogen lifted her chin defiantly.

"Take that, fiend," Imogen challenged, putting her hands on her hips. "Who dost call *me* a child, when he be a child himself? I daresay he hath not the mettle to condescend and meet with me upon the field of battle anon. Hie thee down from thy lofty perch and treat with me, thou crooked rapscallion."

"Forsooth—I should be happy to descend and thrash thee, villain," Basil replied, with flashing eyes and a dreadful, rumbling voice. "If my wound were not something with which I still must contend. Prithee, take thine insults elsewhere, lest ye find thyself face to face with one more puissant and cantankerous than a lion with a thorn in his paw."

Victoria, laughing, broke into applause, causing Imogen's theatrical scowl to dissolve into a grin. Basil flashed his eyebrows at his sister, then returned to his book.

"Don't mind us," Imogen said to Victoria, turning back around to the cluttered piano. "We're always threatening to murder each other."

/*I don't mind,*/ Victoria said, still chuckling. /*I've always thought that's what brothers and sisters do.*/

"Though not quite in that style, I'd imagine," Basil added ruefully—and Victoria glanced at him, realizing he hadn't been reading at all. She met his eyes, her brow furrowing a little.

/*Are you truly in pain?*/

"No, not much anymore," he shook his head, sighing. "Just the occasional stab, which Watson said I should expect. Especially in colder weather."

"Where *are* Watson and Mr. Holmes lately?" Imogen wondered as she started sorting through the books on the piano. "I thought we'd expect to see them once every few days, at least."

/*They're probably on a case,*/ Victoria surmised. /*And...I know Mr. Holmes isn't in the habit of socializing.*/

"He hates it, in fact," Basil added, turning and letting both legs hang over the edge of the shelf.

"I can understand that a man like him might not enjoy small-talk and entertaining," Imogen allowed. "He doubtlessly notices every detail about everyone, which would be maddening. But I thought he'd make an exception for us."

"He might pop round for Christmastime," Basil said lightly, turning a page. "Watson said they might come by."

"Ugh, then we *have* to arrange this room somehow!" Imogen cried, holding up a book in each hand. "It simply *can't* look like this!"

Basil finally started laughing, slammed the book shut, and hopped gracefully down from the shelf.

"All right, all right—stop your whinging," Basil said, waving it off. "Victoria, why don't you and I take these extra lamps and put them in the sliding closet? Now that I'm not writing at the moment, there's no reason to have *that* much light in here."

"Thank you," Imogen sighed heavily. Basil passed her to stand in front of the bookshelf on the other side of the piano, unlatched it and slid it to the left, to reveal a large hidden closet behind the bookshelf. Victoria's memory instantly flashed to the frightening night this past summer, when Basil had fetched her from her room because one of Winchester's henchmen had broken into the house—she and Basil had hidden in the closet while the parlor had been ransacked, and the two of them had been trapped there until Fred Brody had come calling and set them free...

Quickly, Victoria picked up a lamp in each hand and followed Basil, who stepped out of the way for her to pass.

"You may set them on the floor there," he instructed, pointing. She bent down and carefully placed them, then straightened up and turned to see Basil coming in after her with one lamp. She lifted her hands to sign—

Without warning, Basil had slipped his arm around her waist, pulled her into him and pressed his mouth to hers in a deep, fevered kiss that spun her balance and filled her face with heat. She drowned in it, bending back beneath his strength, suddenly surrounded by the scent of him, the feel of his lips, the skin of his face...

He broke the kiss, only to lay more heated kisses to her cheek and the side of her neck. Chills raced all through her body—she smiled and wound her arm around his neck...

"I just realized I hadn't kissed you since this morning," he growled against her neck, and her grin widened.

"Come now, you two—none of that nonsense," Imogen scolded from out in the parlor. "You think you're so clever, ducking out of the work and leaving me all alone."

Victoria giggled into Basil's curls as he kissed her collarbone.

"My sister is a tyrant. Should we tolerate her?" Basil muttered, tightening his hold on her.

"Mhm," Victoria nodded, trying not to swoon.

"Perhaps...we ought to get married tomorrow instead of waiting," Basil purred, pressing his lips to her jaw. "Or—it had better be today. Right now."

Victoria giggled again, then drew back so she could see his face, leaned up and kissed his warm, soft mouth again. He opened his, and pressed deep, kissing her again and again—

She pushed on his chest, parted their lips and withdrew, giving him a saucy but pointed look.

"Right," he cleared his throat, his eyes clearing as he raked his hand through his hair. "Right."

"Basil, I'm going to positively skin you if you don't get back in here," Imogen threatened.

"Well. We can't have that," Basil grinned, a hint of wickedness in his tone as his brilliant eyes wandered all over Victoria's face. She shook her head. He stepped past her and set the lamp down, then started for the door—but leaned in, caught her head in his hand and stole one more staggering kiss before striding back out into the parlor as if nothing had happened.

Victoria, however, had to fight to regain her balance and shake off her giddiness before she reentered—and even then, she knew she was blushing hard, and desperately hoped her hair or collar weren't mussed.

Imogen pretended not to notice. She and Basil were now busily organizing the books on the piano by subject and author, and Victoria set about putting three more lamps in the closet and then shutting it.

Tap, tap, tap!

Sharp, metallic claps of the door knocker.

"Mrs. Butterfield!" Basil bellowed without looking up from his work. "Someone at the door!"

"I heard it, Mr. Collingwood, thank you," Mrs. Butterfield puffed, clattering out from the back kitchen, down the corridor and to the front door, her apron covered in flour. She stopped before opening the inner door, straightened her cap, and then proceeded out to the front door with a pleasant smile on her face. Victoria watched, curious.

She heard voices, but couldn't understand what was said. Just a few seconds later, Mrs. Butterfield came back in with a look of surprise on her face, and bearing a large, decorative envelope.

"Who was it, Mrs. Butterfield?" Basil asked, frowning down at a large black book, whose title Victoria couldn't read at a glance.

"It was a page, sir! And not a page for hire—he was dressed most handsomely, in red velvet!" Mrs. Butterfield cried. "He's sent an invitation!"

"An invitation?" Imogen turned around, immediately interested. Basil set the book down, took the envelope from Mrs. Butterfield, and put on his spectacles. With a flash of his silver letter opener, he had slashed through the envelope and removed the invitation. Victoria stared at it.

It was a half-folded card, the outer cover a lustrous purple with curly gold writing. Basil read the contents intently.

"What is it?" Imogen pressed, eyes fixed on his face. Victoria came up right next to her, just as captivated.

"An invitation to a Christmas party, from a Professor George Rochester," Basil said. "He's written a personal note in here—it isn't printed. He apologizes for the late notice, as the other invitations went out three weeks ago, but it was only yesterday that he discovered the fact that I am *not,* in fact, dead."

/ *Who is he?*/ Victoria wondered. / *Do you know him?*/

"No," Basil shook his head. "He says he attended Cambridge, and he and several friends of his have a great interest in the education of those less fortunate, especially here in London. These friends will be the principle guests at the party. He's heard about my work with private students and thought I might be interested in meeting them."

"Oh," Imogen wilted a little. "So...it's a business party, then."

"I imagine so, but you ought to air out a dress, sister dear," Basil said, striding away from her to sit at his desk, but throwing a playful look at her. "You and James are invited too—and Victoria."

"Oh, huzzah!" Imogen exulted, snatching Victoria by the waist. "Let's get ready together, shall we? I've been dying to play a bit with your hair—may I?"

/*If you will let me play with yours!*/ Victoria answered, giggling again.

"Oh, lord," Basil rolled his eyes—but Victoria could see how secretly delighted he was that his sister liked her.

"Oh, no!" Imogen suddenly gasped, her hand flying to her mouth. "I just realized I don't have anything to wear!"

"So, I'll send your regrets, then?" Basil asked calmly, taking out his stationery from a drawer.

"Of course not!" Imogen cried, as if he'd suggested treason to the crown. "Victoria and I must go *shopping*, that's all."

"Yes, of course, you must," Basil muttered, suppressing a smirk.

Imogen turned and beamed at Victoria, who returned it.

"Shall we go out as soon as we've cleared the parlor?" Victoria laughed.

/*I really think we must!*/

Chapter Two

Saturday, December 16th

Victoria gripped Basil's gloved hand in hers and stepped out into the frosty night. Flurries of snow had begun to fly, catching like fairies in the halos of light that surrounded the lamps that flanked the street. The icy clatter of horse hooves and carriage wheels echoed up and down between the faces of the tall, solemn houses, whose windows glowed with lamplight.

Victoria's feet met the paving stones and she stepped out of the way to allow the Captain to hop down, turn and help Imogen, his wife, out.

Captain James Fleetwood was a tall, noble-looking man, with bright blue eyes, blond hair, and a handsome, serious face. He wore a top hat, tuxedo and black greatcoat, and white gloves. Imogen smiled excitedly at Victoria as she dismounted and took her husband's arm. Imogen wore her fur-lined red cape, her hair done up in curls and sparkling gems—Victoria had dressed it. Victoria herself wore her black coat and muff, and Imogen had done her hair in piles of curls encircled by braids. Basil, like the Captain, wore a tuxedo, top hat, black coat and white gloves. He held his arm out to Victoria, she took it, and they all stepped toward the house before them.

It was a stately, wide, Georgian house, with a brick face

and white frames on the windows and white door; and three worn stone steps leading up to the entrance. All the foggy windows of the house flickered with warm light, and a green wreath tied with scarlet ribbon hung from the door. The group hurried up the steps, and Basil rapped on the knocker.

The next moment, the door opened, and a young, smiling-faced maid in a black dress and white apron and cap dipped a curtsy to them.

"Professor Collingwood," Basil said, producing the glinting invitation he'd received yesterday.

"Yes, sir," the maid beamed at him and gave him another curtsy. "You and your party are expected. Please come in!"

Together, the four of them passed over the threshold and into the house, where a line of servants waited to take their hats, coats and gloves. Imogen revealed her new dress: a sea-foam-green gown with ruffles at the shoulders, and a neckline that showed off the pearly skin of her neck, where a ruby necklace sparkled. As a maid swiftly and politely took Victoria's coat and muff from her, Victoria looked around at the beautifully decorated, glowing entryway, smoothing the skirts of her own new green dress.

The floor was light, polished wood with inlaid designs. Ahead of her across the room waited a broad, sweeping staircase that led up to a landing that then split to either side, where balconies lined both sides of the room, and doors waited to lead to the upper rooms of the house.

Garlands of pine, holly and ivy adorned the bannisters and the pillars that supported the balconies, candles flickered in standing iron candelabras, and a tall Christmas tree stood to one side of the staircase, covered in sparkling glass ornaments and colorful ribbons. The air was filled with the rich scents of pine, cinnamon, cloves, orange zest, candied peel, ginger, and nutmeg, as well as the sounds of lively conversation.

"Beautiful," Imogen praised. "Smells delicious."

"It does indeed," her husband agreed, handing over his hat to a manservant and smiling faintly up at the twinkling chandelier. "I feel transported, don't you? Seems as though our grandfathers would have attended a party like this."

"It does have a rather nostalgic feel, doesn't it?" Basil agreed, glancing around and handing his gloves to the maid. "I wouldn't imagine any change has been made to the house since it was built."

"None at all, in fact—excepting maintenance, of course," came a voice through the broad open door to their left...

And a young man emerged. He looked to be in his late thirties, of an average height, dressed sleekly and fashionably in a very dark red, high-collared coat, embroidered green waistcoat, black trousers and polished shoes, with a sprig of holly pinned to his lapel. He wore an old-fashioned ascot-type white necktie, its tails tucked neatly into the front of his waistcoat. He had handsomely-arranged, luxuriant, wheat-colored curls; an aquiline face, with delicately-Romanesque features, dark eyebrows—and keen, vivid blue eyes that instantly found Victoria's. And in that moment, the striking pierce of his gaze stopped time itself.

Victoria's heart jumped in her chest.

Never in her life had she looked back into such intelligent, indecipherable, acutely-perceptive eyes—not even those of Mr. Sherlock Holmes. For there, in that instant, she seemed to *feel*, rather than see—beneath that attractive veneer of polished elegance and sophistication—a honed, unreachable, almost wild genius. Guarded by the aura of a sphynx. Even as he strode into the entryway, he moved with a powerful, easy grace that implied an athletic body and swift reflexes. He lifted his gaze from Victoria's with calm purpose, turned to Basil, and smiled with the refined charm of a prince. The expression warmed all his features, and lit those intimidating eyes until nothing but enchanting friendliness remained.

"Professor Collingwood," he said—in a voice smooth, tenor and pleasant, with the height of effortless refinement. "I cannot tell you how pleased I am that you are no longer dead."

Basil suddenly laughed—Victoria could feel surprise dart through him.

"Not as pleased as I am," Basil chuckled.

"Professor George Rochester, at your service," the stranger said, proffering his hand and bowing slightly. A signet ring glinted on his forefinger. Basil stepped forward and grasped his hand, and they shook.

"Honored to make your acquaintance," Basil answered. "Thank you for your invitation."

"I'm so gratified you could find the time to come," Professor Rochester said. "Especially at this late hour."

"We are gratified we found ourselves at liberty," Basil answered. "May I introduce my fiancée, Professor Victoria Thulin."

Professor Rochester turned to her, and captivated her gaze once more. For a moment, his direct, fathomless eyes threatened to overwhelm her—until he gave her a bright, engaging smile he seemed to have reserved just for her.

"Madam," he said, taking her offered hand. "I must say that you are a good deal more beautiful than I had imagined—though I first admired the sophisticated and daring beauty of your *mind*, after reading your treatise on your Thulinian language." And he kissed the back of her hand. His lips were warm, his touch gentle and swift.

/*Thank you very much*,/ Victoria signed, feeling herself blush. /*I am honored*./

"Ah," Professor Rochester sighed, canting his head a little at her as his eyebrows came together. "You cannot imagine how deeply I regret that I cannot understand sign language. I do hope you will forgive me, and that one of your party will translate for me, for I have no desire to be bereft of your conversation."

"She said that she thanks you very much," Imogen spoke up. "And that she is honored."

"This is my elder sister, Mrs. Imogen Fleetwood," Basil

motioned to her. "And her husband, Captain James Fleetwood."

"Madam," Professor Rochester took her hand and kissed it as well, then shook hands with the Captain. "I believe I am familiar with your career, Captain. Were you not stationed for some time in northern Africa, and then in the Mediterranean? And your ship's name was *The Pegasus*, was it not?"

"It was indeed," the Captain replied, his attention sharpening. "I wasn't aware that my career would be at all interesting to those living in London."

"Oh, I am enamored with the romance of the sea, and am jealous of anyone who has shared such adventures," Professor Rochester said lightly. "I had a grandfather who told me such fantastic stories—he sailed during the American Revolution, and then the Napoleonic Wars." The Professor glanced at Victoria. "And of course, who has not sat up late into the night with his hair standing on end, reading <u>20,000 Leagues Under the Sea</u>?"

Victoria blinked, blushed again—then managed to return his smile. How could it be? He seemed to *know...*

"I believe you were wondering about the house?" the professor said, turning back to Basil. "And indeed, you are correct. No renovation has been undertaken, except in the addition of water closets and gas, and I have just put in a hot tap, which has made my servants extremely happy, I assure you."

"I would imagine!" Imogen laughed. The professor

returned her spritely look.

"Once one has experienced it, one will never return to a cold tap, mark me," he said, holding up one finger playfully. "But other than that, I have quite a horror of modernity, and the tearing down of the old to make way for the new. I don't mind progress in the way of safety and health, but I hate to see things of beauty and tradition simply steam-rolled and replaced, with no thought to what might be lost in the wake." He considered Basil. "I imagine you're much the same sort of man, Professor Collingwood." He smiled, a little mysteriously. "I daresay you have five or six copies of *Paradise Lost*, but never the desire to be rid of even one of them."

Basil looked back at the professor with just as much intent interest, and smiled a little.

"Well, let's not stand here in this draughty hallway," Professor Rochester clapped his hands together. "Come inside, sit down, and we'll become better acquainted."

He held out his arm to Victoria, and, after glancing at Basil—who nodded—Victoria reached up and took the professor's arm, and allowed him to escort her into the next room.

This high-ceilinged room was filled with well-dressed, middle-aged, scholarly-looking men and their elegantly dressed wives, who all stood near the tall, blazing fireplace or sat in the circles of fine, comfortable furniture, chatting and drinking. This room had also remained decorated in the Georgian style, with distinguished portraits upon the walls, as well as landscapes and seascapes. A pale rug covered the floor, antique tables stood burdened with *hors d'oeuvres*, and more candles twinkled everywhere. In the far corner, another large Christmas tree stood, all a-glitter with candles. The large parlor glowed with the warmth and smells of the season, almost as if perfumed with old-fashioned magic.

Professor Rochester led Victoria to a settee by the front window—heavily curtained—and she sat down.

"Do sit down," the professor instructed, motioning to the other chairs that surrounded the one Victoria occupied. Imogen came and seated herself next to Victoria, and the men made themselves comfortable in the chairs. Last of all, the professor seated himself, and motioned to one of the servants who stood by.

"Would any of you like wassail, or port wine?" he asked them.

"I'll take port," Basil said, and the captain said the same.

"Would you like wassail, Victoria?" Imogen asked her. Victoria nodded, and Imogen asked for another as well. Soon, the servant returned with a tray of their drinks, and soon Victoria held the hot cup in her hands, breathing deep the steaming spices.

"Now, you certainly must be wondering, Professor Collingwood," Rochester said, taking a sip of his own port. "How in the world I heard of you, and why I desired to make your acquaintance."

"Well, in your invitation, you mentioned my work with those suffering with speech impediments," Basil pointed out, resting his elbow on his armrest. "But I don't have any idea how you would have heard of me."

"I have recently become acquainted with some friends of yours, the Brody family," Rochester replied. "Specifically, Lord Fred Brody, and his sister Maria."

Victoria ground her teeth—and at the same time felt a keen stab of pain shoot down through her chest. Basil glanced down at his glass of port, his expression darkening.

"Yes. My family and theirs have been friends for nearly a decade," he said quietly. "Until recently."

"Oh, indeed?" Rochester frowned a little in concern. "I didn't mean to introduce a painful subject. I wasn't aware of any falling out. Lord Fred and Lady Maria certainly didn't indicate there had been one." Rochester watched Basil carefully. "Both spoke very highly of you."

Basil's head came up and he looked at Rochester. Victoria saw something light behind his eyes—something she hadn't seen there in several weeks.

"Indeed?" Basil pressed.

"Yes," Rochester nodded, setting his empty glass on the table and crossing his legs. "We met in the restaurant at the Grand Hotel a week or so ago—I clumsily tripped over something or other, put my hand out to catch myself, and stupidly spilled Lady Brody's glass of wine onto the floor. Instead of having me flogged as a complete imbecile, Lord Brody leaped up to help me regain my footing, and Lady Brody asked if I was quite all right. I ended the evening in their company, talking long into the night."

"Fred has always had a dear heart," Imogen said softly, her brow drawn and her eyes bright as she glanced carefully across at Basil. "It's a pity what happened to both his poor mother...and his brother."

"Yes, I did hear something of that," Rochester nodded gravely, regarding her. "Bad business." He paused a moment, then looked to Basil again. "I had, of course, *heard* of you before my meeting with the Brodys—I am a professor of applied mathematics, and have written a few scholarly papers myself. I try to keep up with other scholars near my own age, even if they aren't studying in my field. I remember noting how prolific you have been, and how broad your research." He sighed shortly. "And then, by way of the papers, I became aware of your apparent death in the Thames. I was deeply grieved that such a genius had been lost." Rochester gazed at Basil softly, as if the pain of that regret had washed through him again—then suddenly smiled and raised his eyebrows. "So...imagine my *delight...*"

Basil chuckled, as did the Captain and Imogen, and Victoria smiled a little.

"Fred told you, then?" Imogen wondered. "That Basil wasn't dead?"

"Yes, he told me a great deal of it," Rochester nodded. "And pointed me toward the newly-published Thulinian language. I bought a copy the very next morning, and read it all that day." He lifted a hand. "Again, I am a mathematician, not a philologist, but I was *fascinated.*"

/ *Thank you,*/ Victoria signed. Rochester gave her a

warm look.

"I believe I understood that one."

"As you've said, you're a mathematician," the Captain pointed out, sitting back in his chair. "But you have an interest in speech impediments?"

"No, not as a science in itself," Rochester shook his head. "I am interested in the outcasts of society—those who have been burdened, by some circumstance of birth or accident, with an impediment to their usefulness, be it a mental or physical disability, or even illiteracy. I believe there are geniuses in every stratum of society, not just the upper classes. Call me a Jacobite for that," he chuckled. "Or even an American! But I am relentlessly intrigued by genius." He turned his head, met Victoria's eyes—and spoke with a quiet, deliberate tone. "I've seen the mind of Newton behind the eyes of a starving farmer. I've seen the hand of God in the fingers of a poor country doctor. And a young woman I knew once...She would have surpassed Euclid. If she had only been able to *see*." He lifted his eyebrows, his voice softening even more as those limitless eyes burned through Victoria's heart.

"Genius should never be locked away, smothered and stifled in dark factories or garrets, or out upon the blasted heath, left to starve and die in obscurity," he murmured. "It must be found, and set free. Given a *voice*. I *live* for this purpose. To find, feed, nurture—and then find solace in the heavenly light it puts off once it can finally make music of its own. It..." He took a breath. It trembled.

"It makes me feel as if I am not so alone after all."

Victoria's breath staggered, and her heart hammered against her chest as a thrill raced through her blood. She tried to swallow, the edge of her tongue aching as her brow knotted. And Professor Rochester held her gaze, as if he knew every thought that had ever passed through her mind.

Quietly, he smiled, and lowered his head. As if he had not meant to let her see so deeply inside of him.

"So..." Imogen ventured. "What do you plan to do with this desire of yours?"

Professor Rochester lifted his head.

"A school, Madam," he replied—with sudden and surprising frankness. "A school for such people as I have described. And—knowing the four of you even as little as I do—I believe the same inspired thought has already occurred to *you*."

Chapter Three

Sunday, December 17th

"I haven't had a chance to ask you, dear," Mrs. Collingwood said, seating herself in her dining room chair as Mrs. Butterfield poured her a small glass of wine. "How was the party last night?"

"Oh, tolerable," Basil sighed, setting a letter down on the tablecloth and taking off his glasses. He sat in his usual place, at the head of the table. "The house was very prettily decorated, the food was decent, and the room was warm."

"You talk like an old maid," Imogen, who sat to his left, commented as she buttered a piece of bread.

"What?" Basil innocently raised his eyebrows at his sister. "Was there something I missed?"

"You quite obviously missed our *host*," Imogen told him.

"Oh, yes indeed, I'd quite forgotten," Basil said lightly, glancing up at the ceiling. "Though I daresay Victoria hasn't—she was smitten."

Victoria, who sat to Imogen's left, opened her mouth in surprise.

/ *What? I wasn't—*/

"Yes, quite," Basil insisted. "In fact, I think I'm in grave danger of being thrown over." And he sent her a twinkling look.

"What nonsense," Imogen muttered, and Victoria

laughed out loud.

Basil, Imogen, Victoria, the Captain, and Mr. and Mrs. Collingwood all sat around the dining room table, beneath the watchful old head of Leonidas the lion, eating their Sunday luncheon.

They had finally all attended church together—and unfortunately had created quite an uproar when Basil Collingwood, a man they had *all* put to rest with *great* ceremony—complete with a marvelous headstone— suddenly came strolling down the center aisle of the church, smiling calmly at everyone, with Victoria on his arm.

Almost everyone who knew him had leaped to his feet and either crowded close to him or backed away in ashen terror. Some people, mostly women the age of Mrs. Collingwood, had broken down weeping—men insisted upon earnestly shaking his hand and grasping his arm, probably to reassure themselves that he was not, in fact, a ghost. The vicar, poor man, had nearly fainted dead away. He had to be sat down in one of the front pews, given some brandy, and talked to at length by Basil himself before he could revive.

Afterward, the scheduled sermon had been abandoned, and Basil had instead sat next to the vicar and answered questions about what had truly happened to him, while the congregation pressed tight in around them. Basil had also thanked them all for the beautiful funeral—which had been described to him at length—and the care that had been taken of his headstone.

Victoria had watched all of this with pleasure, her heart swelling—remembering that very funeral. How she had sat helplessly, listening to Sherlock Holmes and his fellow musicians play "It is Well With My Soul," whilst her own soul felt as if it were being torn apart. Little had she known...

Now, as if the excitement of the morning hadn't ruffled any of them in the slightest, the Collingwoods, the Fleetwoods and Victoria tucked in to a fine luncheon of beef, potatoes, peas, a broth soup and slices of custard, all of them still clothed in their Sunday best.

Mrs. Collingwood, who sat across from Imogen, was a striking woman, with faded blonde hair and intelligent blue eyes. When Victoria had first met her, she had been weighted down with the horrible grief of losing yet another son, her lovely face pale and wan. But now, after finding her son resurrected, her spirits had returned full force, and she was healthy and lively as ever—almost as much as Imogen.

Mr. Collingwood, tall and distinguished, sat to his wife's right. He always looked neat and tidy, with his dark, greying hair and mutton chops trimmed and combed. He had also regained a cheerfulness and energy since his son had returned to him, and often smiled and teased with a subtle and clever wit.

"Your host?" Mr. Collingwood said, glancing at the Captain, who sat at the other head of the table. "He's a professor, isn't he? Was he an exceptional man?"

"He was very amiable and welcoming," the Captain

answered as he cut his meat. "And he seemed very interested in Basil's work, and the concept of a school for those who have learning or communication difficulties."

"Oh, Imogen—you were telling me about that!" Mrs. Collingwood exclaimed, then looked to Victoria. "Did he seem knowledgeable on the subject, Victoria?"

/*Not in technical terms, no,*/ Victoria answered. /*But I feel...*/ She glanced at Basil. /*I feel he understands the difficulties that...people like me...are often forced to live with. And he is sympathetic.*/

"More than sympathetic, I would say," Basil added. "*Empathetic* might be a better word—a trait which I, sadly, have never possessed."

"Tosh," Mrs. Collingwood waved it away. "You are a very kind-hearted young man, Basil. You always have been."

/*I agree,*/ Victoria said, smiling gently at him before picking up her utensils. He returned it.

"What is this professor's background, then, if it isn't in language?" Mr. Collingwood wondered.

"He seems well-off, by the state of his house and servants," the Captain noted. "I doubt his money comes from teaching."

"You're right, James," Basil agreed. "I looked him up last night."

"Oh, indeed?" Imogen said, glancing at him in interest. "What did you find?"

"Professor George Rochester comes from an old family of copper and tin miners—their mines are in Cornwall, where he grew up. He has no noble blood," Basil told them, sipping his tea. "He is unmarried, never has been married; he is an only child, and he inherited this London house from his grandfather."

"Parents are dead?" Mrs. Collingwood prompted. Basil nodded.

"Mm. He was educated at Cambridge, and became a professor of mathematics, and now holds a position at the University of Bolton, which is a technical college. He almost never travels outside of England. And yet..." Basil paused, drumming his fingers on the tablecloth—and Victoria watched his brow darken with thought, and his eyes grow distant.

/ *What?*/ she signed, watching him carefully.

His gaze flicked to hers with instant focus, and his eyes narrowed.

"I could have sworn that there are no traces of Cornish in his speech," he noted quietly.

"That could be overcome on purpose," his mother reminded him. "With a good ear and faithful study."

Basil frowned and shook his head.

"But it can't be eradicated completely. If it isn't in the form of the words themselves, it's in the lilt of the phrasing, and even the word choice, or the sense of humor."

"What, then?" Imogen studied him keenly. "There's something else you noticed, I can tell."

"Yes," Basil mused, gazing at Victoria. "When he was talking to Victoria, telling her about how he felt about the poor and starving geniuses who die, unseen, out in the country..." Basil's frown intensified. "I could have sworn I heard something distinctly *Irish* in his voice."

"Irish!" Mr. Collingwood said in surprise. "You didn't read anything in his background that would indicate he came from Ireland, did you?"

"Not a thing," Basil shook his head. "Which I find...very interesting."

"Indeed so," Mrs. Collingwood agreed. "How puzzling."

"I should like to meet him," Mrs. Collingwood stated. "I am intrigued."

"I'm sure you'll be seeing him," Basil said. "He wants to assist with this school idea of ours. He says he's had the same idea for a long time, but no one has been willing to collaborate with him."

"Sir." Mr. Bradley, the Collingwoods' butler, came into the dining room—holding a tray stacked with *six* letters. He took them to Basil. Basil regarded the butler with surprise.

"What are these?" Basil took them off the tray and shuffled through them—a look of amazement crossing his face. "Well, good lord..."

/ *What? Who is it from?*/ Victoria wondered quickly, as Basil glanced up to see what she said.

"I don't know any of these people," Basil answered, finally fishing out his glasses. "But this one...is in German. And this one is...Russian."

"Russian!" both Mr. Collingwood and Mrs.

Collingwood exclaimed.

"And this one..." Basil held up a beautiful, watermarked envelope. "Is from a Mr. Henry Talbott, caretaker of Lord William Easton."

"For heaven's sake, open one, Basil," Imogen urged, abandoning her meal. Indeed, they all stopped eating, leaning toward him. Basil took the letter opener from the tray and whipped open the first envelope. He hurriedly scanned it.

"This...is from an Herr Oskar Friedrich. He's a German toymaker living here in London, cannot speak English. Professor George Rochester told him to write to me and ask me to take him on as a student." Basil put it back in its envelope and quickly took up the next. He peered closely at it. "This is...from a Miss Alina Aminev, from Dolinsk. She's staying in Surrey with a cousin. She says she hopes I can understand her script, as she cannot speak or write English. Professor Rochester told her to write to me, which she has done...with great reluctance, as she doesn't believe I can be of any use to her at all."

"Hhmf!" Mrs. Collingwood huffed.

Basil put it away, and opened the next envelope.

"This is from a Mrs. Cranehook, the sister of a Lieutenant Harold Gray, who has lost his writing hand in the line of duty. He is despondent and...and suicidal..." Basil's voice lowered. "Because he used to be a writer, a poet, and an artist."

"Poor fellow," the Captain murmured, his eyes bright as

he listened.

"Did Professor Rochester tell this sister to write?" Mr. Collingwood asked.

"He did indeed," Basil mused, putting it back and grabbing the next. "This one was written by Mr. Dickson, the brother of Mary Dickson...whose right-hand fingers were cut off in a mill."

Victoria squeezed her eyes shut and clamped her teeth. Imogen let out a low, tight moan.

"Professor Rochester recommended her case to me," Basil murmured, already reaching for the next envelope. "Ahem. Our Mr. Henry Talbott writes about his ward, Lord William Easton, an orphan with an exceptional learning disorder. He is nine years old but cannot read, write, or even sit still for any length of time. Professor Rochester—"

"—told him to write to you," the Captain finished, and the two men exchanged a look.

"And the last one..." Basil said as he opened and read it. "Is from a Mr. and Mrs. Finlay whose little daughter..." Basil's eyebrows drew together. "...whose little daughter recently suffered an injury which has left her...completely deaf." Basil lifted his head, and looked right at Victoria.

She felt all the heat drain out of her face, and she squeezed her napkin in her lap.

"Well...!" Mrs. Collingwood said breathlessly, glancing around the table. "It sounds as if this school is more than a mere *idea*, after all!"

Chapter Four

/Are you settling into your new house, Imogen?/
Victoria asked.

It had begun to rain that afternoon, preventing the walk through Hyde park they had all planned. So instead, they had all retired to the parlor of Pendywick Place to read, and Mr. and Mrs. Collingwood sat at a small table playing chess. Jack lay on the rug by their feet, sleeping. Queenie, Imogen's cat, had curled up on her lap, and Imogen absently stroked her as she reclined in the chair across from where Victoria sat on the couch.

"Yes, Lark House is charming," Imogen told Victoria. "We can see Grosvenor Square from the window, and of course it's just a short walk from Hyde Park."

/Are you fond of Hyde Park, Captain?/ Victoria wondered. The Captain sat in another chair beside Imogen. He had been reading a blue book of Shakespeare's sonnets without giving it much attention, and he had caught what she said.

"Yes, I enjoy the fresh air, in contrast to the rest of the city. And I'm thinking of getting a dog to come along with us on our walks."

Jack's head instantly came up at the sound of that word, and his tail thumped the rug. The three saw him, and laughed.

"I think you have a volunteer," Basil observed from

where he sat in the window seat, pouring over a copy of the United States Constitution.

"A dog is an invaluable companion, wherever one goes," Mr. Collingwood observed. "I do miss our old Blackie, don't you, dear?"

"What a sweet old dog," Mrs. Collingwood smiled as she moved a pawn. "She loved traveling on trains and ships. Not a bit of trouble."

/*Do Hemsworth and Bessie like the house?*/ Victoria turned back to Imogen.

"Ah, Hemsworth and Bessie..." Imogen sighed, glancing ruefully at her husband, who smiled a little.

/*What?*/ Victoria wondered.

"Well...Bessie is a very dear girl," Imogen said. "I mean, I truly think she is a bright, helpful, competent young woman—"

"Bessie is too young to be in charge of a household," the Captain interrupted frankly. "She's only twenty-two."

Imogen bit her lip in thought as she patted Queenie's head.

"Yes...She is too young. Hemsworth is as solid as he can be, but his duties are limited, of course—and good heavens, there's far too much work for only one maid. Even when I regularly help with the cooking and the linens."

"Do you need me to send Susan to you for a while, dear?" Mrs. Collingwood asked. "Until you can hire more servants?"

"Would you? I think that would be very helpful, thank you, Mum," Imogen nodded. "At least until we can find a cook."

A sharp rap came at the door.

Victoria frowned, twisted around and looked at Basil, who frowned right back at her.

"Who the devil would be mad enough to step out in this weather?" he wondered.

The next second, Mr. Bradley came out of the hallway, opened the inner door and went to the front door. In a moment, he came back, holding the door open, and addressed those in the parlor.

"A Mrs. Fletcher, Miss Richardson and a Mrs. Webster here to see you, Miss Thulin."

Victoria leaped to her feet.

"What?" Basil gasped, standing up too and finding her. "Aren't they—"

/—*Winchester's household,*/ Victoria signed to him, her eyes going wide.

Before she could say any more, the three women came trundling in, having left their wet coats and hats in the entryway. Mrs. Fletcher, black-clad and pressed to perfection despite the weather, her grey hair piled on her head in a simple but classic style, her serious brow furrowed. Mary, Victoria's oldest friend in Oxford, with her fading blonde hair back in a bun, her warm brown eyes finding Victoria immediately as she smiled. Esther, the stout cook, her light-brown hair bound back away from her round, merry face, her thick hands clasped in front of her.

Mr. Collingwood and the Captain immediately got to their feet and bowed to the ladies. And Victoria crossed the room and threw herself into Mary's arms.

"Oh, Miss Thulin!" Mary cried, holding her tight. "How good it is to see you!"

"Ah, Miss—you look lovely!" Esther declared tearfully as Victoria embraced her too.

"You do indeed, Miss," Mrs. Fletcher extended her hand, and Victoria grasped it in both of hers.

"I hope you will forgive us for intruding upon your Sunday afternoon leisure," Mrs. Fletcher said.

"Not at all," Basil stepped forward to stand by Victoria. "You're very welcome. Please come sit down."

"Would you like some tea?" Mrs. Collingwood asked. "I would strongly recommend it, after venturing out in this ghastly weather!"

"Tea would be lovely, thank you," Mrs. Fletcher nodded.

"Mr. Bradley, please ask Mrs. Butterfield to bring tea," Mrs. Collingwood asked.

"Yes, ma'am." And he left.

Victoria backed up and gestured to the couch, and the Captain offered Mrs. Fletcher his chair. Mrs. Fletcher perched on the edge of that chair, and Mary and Esther happily sank down onto the couch, each giving a sigh.

"Victoria, perhaps you'd like to introduce these ladies, and then I will introduce my family," Basil suggested.

Victoria nodded.

/ *These ladies worked in Professor Winchester's household in Oxford,*/ she told them. /*Mrs. Fletcher, the housekeeper, Mary Richardson the maid, and Esther Webster, the cook. They have been my friends since I was eleven years old, and helped to raise me.*/ Victoria found her gaze drifting across their kind faces as they watched her intently, and she felt her throat close. / *They were my family.*/

"Very pleased to meet you all," Mrs. Collingwood said smilingly. "Any friends of Victoria's are welcome at Pendywick Place."

"Mrs. Fletcher, Miss Richardson, Mrs. Webster," Basil said. "These are my parents, Mr. and Mrs. Collingwood, my sister Imogen Fleetwood, and her husband Captain Fleetwood. And of course, my dog Jack, and Imogen's cat Queenie."

"What a handsome dog," Esther remarked with a grin. "I'd love to pet him."

"You may," Basil nodded. "Jack, come here."

Jack immediately hopped up from where he lay and walked over, tail high, to where Basil stood by Esther. Esther immediately bent down and took Jack's head in her hands and waggled his ears with confident vigor.

"Yes, who is a handsome lad?" she cooed at him. "He looks just like an old dog of mine, Mr. Cap. Went everywhere with my dad, following the sheep!"

Jack's tail wagged eagerly as he gazed up into her eyes.

Mary reached out also and patted him, and he soon stood between both ladies, soaking in the attention with pleased dignity. Victoria couldn't keep herself from grinning.

In a few minutes, Mrs. Butterfield came in with the tea tray, which she left in the middle of the parlor, and Imogen had to lift an irritated, growling Queenie over to the Captain so that she could pour out.

"The fire feels lovely," Mary remarked as she took her cup. "The weather truly is horrid."

"Whatever possessed you to venture out into it?" Imogen wondered.

"We truly had no choice," Mrs. Fletcher answered, accepting her own cup from Imogen. "Our train arrived from Oxford in this downpour, and we couldn't very well have pitched camp in the train station. We are due at my sister's house this evening for dinner, and then the hunt begins."

/ *What hunt?*/ Victoria asked.

"Victoria asked 'What hunt?'" Basil interpreted.

"We weren't certain where you were living, Miss, otherwise we would have written," Mary said. "In fact, we came to Mr. Collingwood to inquire as to your whereabouts, so imagine our delight to find you here!" She smiled at the other women. "But yes, we would have told you, if we'd known—but Professor Winchester's house in Oxford has been seized."

"Seized?" Basil repeated, coming around so he could see her better. "Why?"

"Payment of debt," Mrs. Fletcher replied. "Indeed, all three of his properties have been overtaken for that very reason—though we've recently learned that, through some neglect or accident, Heathfell Hall has burned to the ground."

Victoria and Basil looked at each other, but neither of them said anything.

"His house at Bath, too," Esther spoke up. "And all his household staff discharged. His furniture and paintings and silver and other possessions sold to satisfy debts."

"What? I find that hard to believe!" Mr. Collingwood said. "I always thought that the professor was a man of independent means—family wealth, I should say. To whom did he owe these debts? Was he caught up in speculation?"

"Not that I know of, sir," Mary replied. "But Mrs. Fletcher knows more about it than I do."

"I don't believe he speculated," Mrs. Fletcher said. "And I would agree with you, sir—we had always thought that he became a professor out of love for his studies, rather than a need for employment. The other professors at Oxford, those who were not men of means, lived rather humbly, and certainly did not possess *three* houses with large staffs. And frankly, neither Mr. Harrison, the butler, nor myself have the slightest idea about the source of these debts."

Victoria signed again, and Basil translated for her.

"Victoria wants to know if you are, in fact, now out

of work, and if you have taken new positions."

"I have found a position," Mary nodded. "I'll be an upstairs maid here in London at Belgrave Square, in Lord Brody's household."

"Harold, Maria and Fred Brody?" Basil clarified, startled.

"Yes, I believe those are their names," Mary nodded. "Lord Fred Brody and his sister offered me the position—I met them last week when they came to visit a friend in Oxford."

Victoria saw Basil's brow darken, and she felt the same cloud cross her mood. That was now twice recently that Maria Brody had been brought up in a manner strangely connected to themselves. It could be a coincidence—but Victoria didn't really like the feel of it. And clearly, neither did Basil.

"Is that what you mean by 'the hunt,' then?" Mrs. Collingwood asked. "The hunt for positions?"

"Yes, ma'am," Mrs. Fletcher said. "And though I have no right to ask for it, as this was meant to be a social call to Miss Thulin, we would be greatly obliged if you would keep us in mind, if any of your acquaintance should be searching for servants. I myself have had twenty years' experience as a housekeeper, and Mrs. Webster has had thirty years' experience in the kitchen—and both of us have only worked in two different households all our lives."

/*Imogen,*/ Victoria signed carefully to her friend. /*I know you don't know these ladies, but you can trust me when I say—/*

"I trust you implicitly," Imogen interrupted her—and turned directly to Mrs. Fletcher. "Mrs. Fletcher, Mrs. Webster—I would be more than happy to offer you employment."

Both women stared at her.

"Mrs. Fleetwood—!" Mrs. Webster gasped.

"You may not believe it, but we were discussing this very subject when you arrived," the Captain added. "We've just moved into a new house near Grosvenor Square, called Lark House, and we are gravely under-staffed, with only a butler and a young upstairs maid."

"You would be offering us a great deal of relief if you would accept," Imogen said. "I'd be happy to start you at fifty pounds a year, Mrs. Fletcher, and Mrs. Webster, I would start you at forty pounds a year." Imogen glanced at Victoria. "You raised and fed and clothed my future sister—and if she speaks highly of you, that is a good enough reference for my tastes. Will you accept?"

"Why...Yes, Mrs. Fleetwood, without hesitation!" Mrs. Fletcher cried. "Thank you so very much!"

"I'll gladly accept, too, ma'am," Esther nodded happily. "Thankee."

"And Mary—I certainly would have hired you as well, if you weren't already employed," Imogen stated. "If your situation isn't to your liking at the Brody house, know that my door is always open to you."

"Thank you, ma'am," Mary said, blushing. "I'm most

grateful."

The three women stayed for tea, and their discussion drifted toward the Collingwoods' traveling adventures, and the Captain's varied career. They asked many eager questions, and Mr. and Mrs. Collingwood were happy to provide them with tales about Italy, France, Germany and Spain, and the Captain readily described to them what life was like at sea.

When the clock struck half past three, the ladies arose to take their leave, and Imogen gave Esther and Mrs. Fletcher her card, having written her new house address on it.

"Please come tomorrow, if you would, at ten in the morning," Imogen bid them. "And I will show you around the house."

Again, Mrs. Fletcher and Esther thanked her and the Captain profusely, and Victoria promised she would see Mary, as they were friends with Fred Brody. Mr. Collingwood then told Mr. Bradley to order a cab for the women, as he wouldn't hear of them walking anywhere in this weather. The ladies protested, but to no avail, and Mr. Bradley ordered them to stay inside until he had found the cab. After embracing Victoria again, the three women departed, and Victoria promised to see them soon.

"Well, that was fortuitous," Imogen mused, gazing at the front door.

"For them, especially," Basil remarked, putting his hands in his trousers pockets. His voice lowered. "I naturally assumed that Winchester's death would cause his household to be scattered…But I've no idea why all his assets would be seized for debts."

"Did he have any family?" Mrs. Collingwood asked.

/No, not that I know of./ Victoria shook her head. */He had a sister, but she died without children almost ten years ago./*

"So, it wouldn't have been seized to satisfy another family member's debts," Mr. Collingwood concluded. "This was a consequence of his own actions."

Tap, tap, tap.

"Good heavens, more visitors?" Mrs. Collingwood exclaimed. "Has everyone gone mad?"

This time, instead of waiting for Mr. Bradley, the Captain, carrying a disgruntled Queenie, opened the inner door and went to the front. Almost immediately, male voices rang out—

And in swept Sherlock Holmes and Dr. Watson, taking off their coats and hats as they came.

Sherlock Holmes, a young, striking and handsome man, with piercing grey eyes and dark hair, seemed unusually vivid today—as if the rain and gloom enlivened his very spirit. Indeed, a subtly mischievous and satisfied smile graced his intelligent mouth as he entered and handed his hat to Mr. Bradley, who had arrived to help. Holmes wore a crisp black suit, his silver watch chain sparkling in the firelight.

Dr. Watson, a good deal less enthusiastic than his dramatic friend, wore tweeds, his shoulders braced against the cold. He sighed as he took off his hat and ran his hand through his hair. Dr. Watson was handsome too, with his lighter hair and trimmed mustache, and finally appeared to be gaining a healthy weight back, as he had lost so much due to his wound and illness in Afghanistan. He immediately came to stand in front of the fire and put his hands behind his back to warm them—and Jack went to him straightaway, and sat on his feet.

"Good afternoon, cousin," Holmes greeted Basil fluidly, his smile increasing as he extended his hand. Basil, chuckling, shook his hand.

"What the devil are the two of you doing out in the rain?" Basil demanded.

"It's just the sort of weather he likes," Watson grumbled. "I told him we'll both catch our deaths, but he didn't care."

"Oh, come now, Watson," Holmes scoffed. "A bit of water cannot make one sick."

"A chill can, mark my words," Watson retorted. "But then again, you're never ill, are you?"

Holmes, cheerfully ignoring him, inclined his head to the others in the room.

"Mr. and Mrs. Collingwood, good afternoon," he said. "And Miss Thulin, how are you?"

/*Very well, thank you,*/ she replied. /*How are you?*/

"Tolerable lately, tolerable," Holmes answered. "We've just finished a case yesterday—grim business."

"A former MP was beheaded by his wife," Watson said,

raising his eyebrows. "In his castle in Scotland. We've only just gotten off the train this morning."

"I'm sorry, Watson is trying to distract me with gruesome details while I neglect my manners." Holmes turned to Imogen, and his expression softened. "How are you, Mrs. Fleetwood?"

"I'm well, Mr. Holmes," Imogen smiled at him and extended her hand. He took it and clasped her fingers for a moment, before releasing her and turning to the Captain.

"And you, sir? I trust you're enjoying London?"

"It's a good deal foggier and rainier than I'm used to," the Captain replied. "But at least the parks are nearby."

"You prefer the open air, don't you, Captain?" Watson remarked cheerfully. "I'd adore a country practice myself, maybe somewhere in Yorkshire."

"Oh, Watson, you'd die of boredom," Holmes said flatly—and Watson rolled his eyes.

Victoria suppressed a snicker.

"Please sit down, gentlemen," Mrs. Collingwood invited.

"If it's quite all right, I'll stay here in front of the fire," Watson said. "I'm chilled to the bone."

"I'm afraid my colleague is still quite acclimated to a hotter climate," Holmes noted as he smoothly took a seat on the couch. The Captain seated himself in the chair he had occupied before, while Victoria sat in her chair, and Basil sat down beside Mr. Holmes.

"Is this simply a social call, Mr. Holmes?" Mr.

Collingwood asked. "Or is there something we can help you with?"

"I never miss an opportunity to visit Pendywick Place," Holmes stated. "But I confess that this particular visit is driven by a great deal of curiosity."

/ *What about?*/ Victoria wondered.

"Your school," Holmes told her frankly. "It's all over town that you, Basil, and Mr. and Mrs. Fleetwood—with the help of a Professor Rochester—are starting a college for those struggling with all manner of difficulties in communication."

"Ha! How can that be?" Imogen cried. "We only just discussed it seriously for the first time last night!"

"Nevertheless, it is being talked about in every circle," Holmes replied. "This Professor George Rochester appears incredibly well-connected."

"Do you know anything about him?" Basil asked. Holmes met Basil's keen gaze with one of his own.

"No more than your social register tells you," he said. "And doubtless, you know even more than I do, as I have never met the man."

"Nor have I," Watson spoke up. "Though his reputation is a respectable one."

"We did discuss it with him last night," Basil admitted. "And this morning, I received several letters from students who are interested in joining."

Holmes' gaze cast downward, and his brow furrowed.

"What is it?" Imogen asked him, watching his

expression.

"Nothing at all, madam," he glanced at her. "Simply storing all these facts away, should they prove to be useful later." He took a breath, and looked up at Victoria. "Do you indeed plan to open such a college?"

/ *Yes,*/ Victoria nodded. / *I'm very interested in it, and I believe we can help many people, especially children.*/

"Do you have a building?" Watson asked.

"No," Basil turned to him. "Do you think we might need one?"

"You might consider it. It's always a good idea, in my experience, to be able to retreat from one's work into the sanctuary of home," Watson said. "Leave the mess at the office, if you will. I think our landlady, Mrs. Hudson, would agree." He gave a pointed look to Holmes, who only heaved a labored sigh and looked somewhere else. Imogen laughed—and Holmes clearly suppressed a knowing smile, and didn't look at her.

Then, he glanced over the tea tray.

"You've just had guests, then? Three women, by the state of the tea," he noted. "Working class—servants, most likely in a bachelor's household?"

"How on earth—" Watson exclaimed.

"Oh, the tea, Watson—you can tell almost everything about a person by her tea," Holmes said dismissively, then looked at Imogen. "Interviewing staff for your new home?"

"Well—we *did* hire two of them, yes," Imogen looked at her husband, startled. "But that wasn't the reason for their visit!"

"No?" Holmes looked to Victoria, his brow furrowing. "Forgive my curiosity—it's an incurable fault of mine."

/ *They were members of Professor Winchester's former household,*/ Victoria told him. / *The housekeeper, a downstairs maid and the cook. They came to visit me—they are staying in London, looking for new positions.*/

"New positions?" Watson repeated. "Oh—I suppose, since Winchester died—"

"Yes, but not only that," Basil said, his voice low. "They told us that all of Winchester's assets—his houses, his furniture, everything—have been seized to pay *debts.*"

Holmes looked at him sharply, all his levity vanishing.

"Debts?" he said carefully. "Belonging to a relative, an heir?"

/ *No,*/ Victoria said. / *He had no family.*/

"Intriguing," Holmes mused—then his attention flashed to Victoria. "Did he play the markets, or gamble?"

/ *No, neither,*/ Victoria said. / *At least...not that I know of.*/ She shrugged painfully. / *But...there is a great deal I never knew about that man.*/

"Of course," Holmes murmured. "So...Our dear Professor Winchester isn't yet finished playing mischief upon us."

"Mischief, what do you mean?" Basil demanded.

"Perhaps nothing," Holmes offered him a faint smile, but his thoughts were clearly racing ahead elsewhere. "With your permission, I'll look into this, if I may."

"What, what is it?" Imogen sat up, her eyes fixed on him. He looked at her directly, and raised his eyebrows.

"I would simply prefer that this very formidable enemy of ours, now that he is dead, keeps no more secrets from us," he answered plainly. "Even when a snake's head is severed, it may still bite." Abruptly, he stood to his feet, and bowed to them, then headed to the door. "Come, Watson—Mrs. Hudson has doubtlessly cleaned and straightened Baker Street during our absence, and I'm certain I shan't be able to find a thing."

"Thank you for letting us come in and warm up," Watson smiled at them. "Do come visit us, sometime."

"Truly?" Imogen said, surprised. "You want us to come to Baker Street?"

Holmes spun around to look at her, as if utterly confused.

"Mrs. Fleetwood," he said, with unusual earnestness. "You are welcome to come to Baker Street whenever you desire, without any notice at all."

"Well then—James and I will be happy to come," Imogen grinned. "I've never paid a visit to a detective's home before."

"It's no different from any other flat, I assure you," Watson joked. "Except that there are papers all over the floor, and it smells of gunpowder."

"Nonsense, Watson," Holmes swept to the door and found his coat and hat. "Good day to you all!"

"Good afternoon!" Watson added, and with that, the

eccentric pair of colleagues headed out into the rain, leaving the occupants of Pendywick Place to discuss the day's events for hours into the evening.

Chapter Five

Monday, December 18th

Mercifully, the weather cleared the next morning, the sun came out and the temperature warmed. Imogen was able to meet Mrs. Fletcher and Esther at Lark House, show them their quarters and set them to work before coming over to Pendywick Place for luncheon.

Then, after they had eaten, Victoria, Imogen and Mrs. Collingwood were able to venture out into the city to Christmas shop at Leadenhall Market. Once Victoria had told Imogen about her trip last year, with Fred, Imogen had been relentless in promoting a similar trip to her mother, until Mrs. Collingwood had had no choice but to give in to her daughter's enthusiasm.

The three ladies bundled up and squeezed themselves into a hansom cab, and Victoria thoroughly enjoyed the drive through London in the daylight. The streets were even busier than usual, and, since it was so near Christmastime, she lost count of how many people were carrying bundles of seasonal greenery like holly and pine branches down the walkways, decking out their storefronts, and hanging wreaths. Many more toted wrapped packages and parcels, some in brown paper, others with colorful ribbons. The street criers raised their voices over the noise of the carriages, advertising their wares with lilting songs and pleasant phrases, like:

"Will ye buy any milk today, madam? Whitest milk in town, madam! Will you buy any milk today?"

"Red ribbons, blue ribbons, all the colors of ribbons! Come buy a ribbon, miss, for only half a penny!"

"Extra, extra! Read all about it! Archbishop of Canterbury Gets Lavish Funeral!"

"Rosemary and bay! Will you buy any rosemary? Will you buy any bay? Rosemary and bay!"

And more than once, Victoria caught sight of groups of carolers heartily singing, with cups in their hands:

Hark! The herald angels sing
Glory to the newborn King!
Peace on earth, and mercy mild
God and sinners reconciled!

And,

"Here we come a'wassailing, upon the leaves so green!
Here we come a'wandering, so fair to be seen!
Love and joy come to you, and to you glad Christmas, too!
And God bless you, and send you happy new year!
And God send you a happy new year!

"How lovely to be in London at Christmastime," Imogen sighed. "Basil told us some of what you did last year, Victoria—did you manage to be very festive?"

/Oh, yes—as much as we could be when we only had a day to prepare!/ Victoria laughed. */We had a tree, and garlands, and Mrs. Butterfield and her daughter Elsie and I made Christmas dinner, and we got little penny parcels to put under the tree, which we opened on Christmas Eve, and I made Basil a scarf—/*

"Oh, yes, that *scarf,*" Imogen smiled knowingly. "I daresay that's when he fell in love with you, Victoria."

Victoria gave her a wide-eyed look.

"It's true," Mrs. Collingwood assured her. "From then on, he scarcely wrote to us about anything but you. We had no idea what state the house was in, how his students were, or if any of our acquaintances were still alive. We were delighted."

Victoria laughed, feeling her heart warm.

They continued on their journey until they reached Leadenhall Market, and the three ladies climbed out of the hansom and joined the throng of people pressing in and out of the markets. Now, the usual noise of the street was accompanied by jingling bells and even more singing, as carolers congregated on the corners here. The narrow tunnel of buildings leading to the spectacular Christmas tree that stood in the arch of the market, provided a cathedral of sound for singing voices—and the sudden, enveloping magic of the season made Victoria grin like a little girl. She glanced over at Imogen...

To see her friend standing there, her lovely face upturned, shining tears filling her eyes.

"Oh, Mumma," she whispered, her lip trembling. "I'm...I'm so happy we've come home."

"So am I, my dear," Mrs. Collingwood said, just as tearfully, as she wrapped her arm around Imogen's right. "Thank you for persuading me."

"And thank *you* for putting it into my head," Imogen smiled at Victoria through her tears and quickly looped her arm through Victoria's. "Now—let us shop until we simply collapse. Shall we?"

/ *Yes!*/ Victoria signed. Mrs. Collingwood laughed. And together, arm in arm and in stride, they were off.

They visited every shop—dozens of shops Victoria had never seen before, selling dried goods, flowers, fabrics, toys, hats, clothing, candies, potted plants, spices, candles, jewelry; live animals like birds, cats, lizards and monkeys; stationery and pens, men's shaving accessories, ladies' beauty items for skin and hair; and all manner of foods. They purchased presents for Basil, Mr. Collingwood, and all their servants, as well as several friends and neighbors. They even managed to shop some for each other, commanding each to "look away!" whenever they were making a choice. They ordered their purchases to be delivered to Pendywick Place, so they would not have to carry anything.

"Oh, my word!" Imogen suddenly gasped, as she jumped to a halt in front of a shop window. "Mother, look!"

"What is it?" Mrs. Collingwood pressed closer, as did Victoria...

"There it is!" Imogen pointed. "It's your language, Victoria— *Thulinian!*"

And so it was. Right there, displayed in a book shop's display window, along beautiful copies of classics and new releases alike, was a lovely little red book with a gold crown stamped on the center of the cover. Victoria's eyes welled up with tears that blurred her vision. She couldn't read the words on the front—but she didn't need to.

"What a lovely little volume," Imogen said as she wrapped her arm around Victoria's waist. "Just look at that. Sitting there right next to Shakespeare's Sonnets. Almost too pretty to wrap."

Victoria sniffed, smiling shakily, and swiped at her eyes. Imogen leaned over and kissed her forehead.

"I'm getting three copies," she decided crisply, and strode straight to the shop door and went inside.

"I need at least four," Mrs. Collingwood decided. "To send to my sister's family. Are you coming, Victoria?"

/ I'll be in in a moment,/ Victoria signed to her.

"Take your time, dear," Mrs. Collingwood smiled at her, and followed her daughter.

As the door shut, Victoria turned back to the book in the window, seeing her own faint reflection against the glass, framing the brand-new volume. And memories echoed through her mind.

Being a young, innocent student of *everything* she could get her hands on, ravenously devouring languages as if she couldn't get enough...

Getting the idea from Mary that she ought to conceive of a language all her own...

Writing and writing, far into the night, over and over, working out all the words and meanings and arrangements...and exceptions...

Proudly showing it off to her guardian and mentor, Professor Winchester one warm, spring morning. Basking in the glow of his stunned admiration, his speechless awe at what she had accomplished...

The carriage ride to Cambridge, in the dark.

Violence. Blood. Cold. The claws of death sinking into her arms and legs...

The farmer's house. Mutely nursing them through fever, just as they had nursed her back from the brink of oblivion...

Hurrying through the London fog to Pendywick Place, wondering all the time how she was going to make this forbidding young man understand her...

The Christmas ball at Hampton Court, where Winchester had threatened to kill Basil if she pursued the language any further...

Learning how to speak again, through sign language. Practicing and practicing how to read once more, and to write...

Losing Basil in the Thames. Finding him again, at Baker Street...

Long hours at Heathfell Hall, with Basil, by the light of a lamp, recreating the entire thing, line by line, exception by exception...

Meeting the Queen of England herself. At Buckingham Palace. Hearing her say that she would publish the work, and have it disseminated all over England, so that Winchester's plans would be useless, and Victoria's work would be recognized—

"Miss?"

Victoria jumped, turning quickly to the right—

A tall, handsome man with a trimmed, reddish beard, and a grey slouch hat stood there, smiling quietly at her. He wore a grey coat with the collar turned up, and a thick scarf—as if, even in the shelter of the Market, he was too cold. He had vivid and penetrating green eyes, and an abundance of freckles—as if he had recently been in a very hot and sunny climate. His face seemed a bit thin for his age, giving Victoria the thought that perhaps he had been forced to live through something harsh and difficult. When she met his gaze, his smile gentled and warmed, and he inclined his head to her.

"May I ask if you know the author of that book, there—the one in the window?"

Victoria's mouth opened, and she reflexively started to sign...

Then stopped helplessly.

He blinked, but didn't blush or turn away. Instead, he inclined his head again.

"Professor Thulin, I presume?"

Victoria gasped, and stared at him.

He chuckled, and his face gained even more amiability.

"Forgive me—I am Professor Xavier Churchill," he said, putting a gloved hand on his chest. "And I am honored to meet you. Please—use your sign language. I myself am a professor of languages at the University of London."

/*How did you know who I was?*/ she managed.

"I was passing by and I overheard your friends say your language was in the window," he answered. "I hope you don't mind my intrusion—I simply couldn't help myself. I have actually been screwing up the courage to write to you for several weeks, now."

/*Really?*/ Victoria said, still marveling at being able to communicate with a complete stranger. /*How can I help you?*/

"Ever since I got my hands on a copy of your language, I have been teaching my students Thulinian," he began eagerly. "They ate it up more ravenously than anything I'd given them before. Now, they're off on holiday, and I've just been possessed by this idea of creating a curriculum for a class on modern *invented* languages. And I..." He took a breath, and suddenly gained an air of a tender man frightened of rejection. "I would be *so* very honored if I could commission another language from you. Or...as many languages as you are willing to write."

Victoria stared at him again, stunned down to her core.

/*Professor...*/ she struggled.

"Churchill," he said earnestly.

/*Professor C,*/ she said, smiling a little as she used an

abbreviation. */I am incredibly honored that you would ask me—/*

"No, not at all," he held up a hand. "*You* would be doing me the greatest honor. In fact, the reason I haven't written is that I felt so foolish, so presumptuous, for even *thinking* that you might deign to do such a thing for me. But now that I see you..." He gazed at her for a moment. "And I see not only how intelligent, but how lovely and kind-hearted you are, it's given me a bit of courage I didn't have before."

Victoria laughed, feeling her face heat up.

/ Thank you, Professor. I confess, I...I haven't thought of continuing that line of work, since it's recently become a great deal more difficult than it was.../

"I understand," he nodded. "But I also intend to pay you for your efforts and your time. And I would of course be at your disposal should you ever need help with any project of your own."

/I.../ Victoria began—and then inspiration flashed through her mind.

A professor of language. And he could understand *hand-language.*

And they were about to try to build a *school...*

*/May I consider your offer? Talk about it with my fiancé?"*Victoria asked quickly. */Because, of course, he would need to help me if I were to undertake this project—/*

"Of course, of course!" Professor Churchill said quickly. "Here is my card!" And he reached in his coat and pulled out a calling card, and handed it to her. "Please send me word as soon as you can. I'll be waiting sleeplessly until I hear from you."

Victoria grinned at him as she took it, and he smiled happily back.

"I shan't detain you any longer." He tipped his hat to her. "Merry Christmas!"

/*Merry Christmas!*/ she replied, and he hurried off into the crowd, and Victoria watched him go.

Chapter Six

Imogen opened the oaken box on her bed, and held the lid quietly in both hands as she looked down at its contents. For a long moment, she just stood there, brow furrowed—then glanced up and around her new bedroom in Lark House.

White walls, bare wooden floor. The four-poster bed stood in front of her, snugged into the northeast corner of the room. At its foot, a tall window looked down into the side street. She had yet to hang curtains. The white fireplace stood in the west wall, and a healthy fire burned there, warming the empty space.

Imogen took a deep breath. Then, carefully, she reached inside the box and unwrapped a framed photograph from its papers. A circular portrait of a little boy with blond curls. Her little brother, David.

For a long time, she held it there, looking into his faded eyes. Then, she carried it over to the fire and set it up on the mantlepiece. One by one, she unwrapped pictures: her parents' wedding photograph; a family picture taken when she was eighteen, which included her mother, father, and Basil. Her own wedding picture, with her handsome husband dressed in his military finest standing beside her, in her white gown and veil. And of course, the portrait of her cat, Queenie.

Imogen stepped back and put her hands on her hips,

looking over her work. Her mind wandering into the past, over years of travel on the continent...unpacking over and over, only to pack again...

"Mistress?"

Imogen jumped—and blinked, surprised to find tears in her eyes. She quickly smiled as she turned to the black-clad Mrs. Fletcher, who stood uncertainly in the doorway.

"Forgive me, ma'am," Mrs. Fletcher said quickly.

"No, it's all right, Mrs. Fletcher," Imogen assured her, quickly swiping away her tears, straightening up and braving another smile.

"Are you all right?" Mrs. Fletcher asked.

"I...Yes, actually," Imogen said, taking another deep breath as she freshly considered the portraits on the mantle. "I've just realized that I'll never have to put these pictures back in that box." She faced Mrs. Fletcher. "This is the very first house I can truly call my own. And I've decided I shan't ever sell it. I'm determined to pass it to one of Victoria and Basil's children."

"Not your own children, ma'am?" Mrs. Fletcher tilted her head.

"Oh, I...No, unfortunately," Imogen shook her head. "I've been to several doctors, none of them can tell me what's the matter with me. But I've never been able to conceive a child."

"Oh. I'm so sorry, ma'am," Mrs. Fletcher said quietly, watching her. Imogen fought back that familiar ache in her chest and lifted her chin.

"That's all right," she said cheerfully. "Queenie is quite demanding enough for me."

"I daresay," Mrs. Fletcher smiled gently.

"Erm...Did you have another question?" Imogen asked, remembering herself. "I know this is a lot to get used to, on the very first day—"

"No ma'am," Mrs. Fletcher shook her head. "I came to tell you that two gentlemen have come to see you. I told them that the Captain is out for the day, but they said they wished to speak to you."

"Who are they?" Imogen frowned, stepping toward her.

"A Mr. Holmes and Dr. Watson," Mrs. Fletcher answered.

Imogen's smile instantly became genuine, and warmth dispelled the ache in her heart.

"Oh, of course! In the future, Mrs. Fletcher, you may admit them at any time of day or night—they are dear friends of my family."

"Yes, ma'am," Mrs. Fletcher answered quickly, and followed Imogen out of the room and into the airy hallway, then down the curved, sweeping staircase that led to the entryway.

Imogen had loved this Georgian house from the moment she saw it, because the previous owner had painted almost all the interior *white*. Though it made for some extra work for the servants—washing the walls at least once a week—it made the whole house feel bright, open and fresh, as well as being a blank canvas for all the Italian and French art she and the Captain had collected on their travels.

"Dr. Watson, Mr. Holmes!" Imogen called, as soon as she saw them down below. "So glad you could come! What do you think of Lark House?"

Mr. Holmes instantly looked up at her as she descended, his lightning grey eyes finding hers—and warming to the shade of an autumn sky. He wore a pristine black suit and tie, his dark hair slicked back. He gave her a quiet, familiar smile.

Dr. Watson turned from admiring the painting of a landscape that hung by the door, and gave Imogen a beaming grin. He wore walking tweeds—very different from the fashion of the city—but they suited him best of all.

"Good afternoon, Mrs. Fleetwood," Mr. Holmes greeted her smoothly. "The house is lovely."

"Splendid, I should say," Watson remarked, looking around. "What an elegant entryway and staircase."

"I daresay that's one of the reasons Mrs. Fleetwood chose it, Watson," Holmes glanced at his friend. "That, and the tall ceilings, large windows, and light-colored paint on the walls gives one a sense of almost being outdoors, while allowing creativity and freedom in decoration."

"Ha!" Imogen laughed, amazed, as she arrived in front of them. "You've read my mind, Mr. Holmes."

His smile increased, but he glanced down.

She held out her hand to Dr. Watson, who happily shook it. Then, she reached out to Holmes. He paused, but finally grasped her fingers in a far more careful manner than she'd expected—and only briefly.

"May we speak to you for a few moments?" he asked her, glancing through the door to his right, into the parlor. "We won't take much of your time."

"You may take as much time as you would like," Imogen assured him. "I don't have any engagements, and my husband is away from home on business. In fact, if you aren't otherwise occupied, you may certainly dine with me."

"Forgive us, but—" Holmes started.

"We accept," Watson cut in. "Holmes hasn't eaten anything today, and I myself have only had a small breakfast."

Imogen saw disconcertion tighten Holmes' brow for a moment, and he avoided looking at either of them. Purposefully, Imogen put her hand on Holmes' arm.

"Please don't feel as if you must," she said, watching him. "But I would be grateful for the company."

"Of course," Holmes said quietly, and met her eyes for just a moment. But she took the opportunity to smile.

"Please, come in," she invited, and stepped through the door into the parlor.

A pale green rug with fringe covered the floor, and double windows in the south wall, with a window seat and hung with lace curtains, looked out upon the wide street and the park beyond. The fireplace stood against the north wall, blazing and warm. But Imogen had arranged the French-style Regency chairs and couch around the rug instead, so that she could look out the windows and watch the traffic of London go by, as well as the birds fluttering through the trees.

"Please sit down," Imogen invited, taking the furthest chair and seating herself. "Mrs. Fletcher, could you bring tea for the three of us?"

"Yes, ma'am," Mrs. Fletcher turned and headed toward the kitchen, while Holmes and Watson entered. Watson sat down in the chair directly across the rug from Imogen, and Holmes chose the end of the couch closest to her. He threw back is coattails and gracefully sat, setting his elbow on the armrest, his brow furrowing as he looked straight out the window, as if he were somewhere else. Imogen found herself fascinated by his graceful, catlike movements.

"Tell me again, Mr. Holmes," Imogen said thoughtfully as she studied him. "How are you and I related?"

"Not related at all, in fact," he said quickly, turning his sharp attention to her. "Not by blood. We are, in reality, only related by marriage. My mother had a much older sister who married your great uncle—your mother's uncle, to be exact."

"Oh, yes, of course," Imogen nodded. "May I be permitted to call you 'Sherlock,' then? I don't recall if I've ever asked your permission—it may have slipped out before this."

Holmes looked at her, as if surprised, his mouth opened—

And he nodded.

"Certainly," he agreed. "If you wish."

"And please—you may call me John," Watson added. "I almost never see my brother anymore, and I miss hearing my given name."

"You have a brother?" Imogen sat up. "Where does he live?"

"In the west, somewhere," Watson sighed, clasping his hands together as a cloud passed over his face. "He hasn't been well for some time, and, both our parents being dead, I'm afraid my long campaign in Afghanistan served to cut us off from each other. He may resent me for it, I don't know. But I'm truly sorry for it."

"It isn't your fault, Watson," Sherlock glanced at him. "Your country required your service. You had no choice in the matter."

"That doesn't make it any easier, unfortunately," Imogen said quietly, gazing at Watson. "Sometimes, having no choice in the matter makes it worse."

She felt Sherlock considering her, and Watson smiled kindly back at her. She could tell he understood what she meant.

Just then, Mrs. Fletcher returned with the tea tray, and she wheeled it in front of Imogen.

"Thank you, Mrs. Fletcher," Imogen said, as she picked up the pot and set to pouring the tea for her guests.

"Mrs. Fletcher, would you be so good as to stay for a moment?" Sherlock asked. "We'd like to ask you a few questions about your previous employer."

"Of course, sir," Mrs. Fletcher said.

"You may sit down, Mrs. Fletcher," Imogen nodded to the window seat, and the woman seated herself very neatly and elegantly, folding her hands in her lap. Imogen hid her swell of pleasure and gratitude that such a woman had joined her household.

"Mrs. Fletcher," Sherlock began, watching her with a penetrating, hawk-like regard. "Dr. Watson and I are looking into a bit of a mystery for our friends, the Collingwoods—and Victoria Thulin—that concerns Professor Harcourt Winchester. Three questions still remain unanswered in this case, and they do not sit well with me. If you can help me answer them, I would be most grateful."

"I will help however I can, sir," Mrs. Fletcher said firmly. "Before he died, I learned that my master was an exceedingly-dishonest man, and I no longer have any loyalty to him."

"Indeed," Sherlock nodded. "May I ask if you know who is in possession of Professor Winchester's official documents? His bank ledgers, his will, his deeds, et cetera?"

"Yes, sir, he employed a solicitor," Mrs. Fletcher said. "A Mr. Boyle, of Boyle, Carter and Blast, here in London. I'm certain he would have copies of everything, if not the originals."

"Make a note of that, Watson," Sherlock said, as Watson took out his notebook and began to scribble.

"You think that, if we could get a look at those documents, we might find out what happened with his finances, that caused him to lose all his property after his death?" Watson supposed.

"They may enlighten us, yes," Sherlock said.

"And what are your other questions?" Imogen asked him.

"What would be the most logical following question, Mrs. Fleetwood?" Sherlock turned toward her. "If we indeed discovered that Professor Winchester *knew* he was in dire financial straits?"

"The most logical?" Imogen said. "Well, that would be: what did he plan to do about it? What action was he taking to prevent his property from being seized? And, if he *was* taking action..." Imogen suddenly went cold. "...did it have to do with selling Victoria's language...?"

Sherlock Holmes was now looking at her with vivid intensity, as if something had just flashed through his mind and sunk into his bones.

And Imogen instantly knew she was right. She sat forward, leaning toward him, her own mind flying.

"And the *next* question is," she went on, her heart picking up. "Did the selling of the language come to him naturally, or was it presented to him in such a way as to be his only option?" She gestured as she thought. "If he didn't sell the language, he would lose everything? Victoria has often said how well she was treated in his house—like his own daughter. She even believed he loved her. Could it be that...someone *else* inspired him to attack her and steal the language, out of desperation?"

Sherlock's eyes burned as the two gazed at each other,

and the weight of what she'd just said stunned Imogen to her core.

"You're right, ma'am," Mrs. Fletcher said—and both Imogen and Sherlock blinked, and turned immediately to her.

"Indeed?" Sherlock prompted

"Yes, sir," Mrs. Fletcher affirmed, looking suddenly stark and pale. "Professor Winchester first told me that he was thinking of having Miss Thulin's language published by the university, in a scholarly journal. But then, one evening after a party, he walked home and stayed up late in the sitting room, just staring into the fire. When I asked him if he was well, he said, 'Yes, Mrs. Fletcher, I'm well. I'm in receipt of a proposal concerning Victoria's new invention.' I asked him what sort of proposal it was." She hesitated. "In usual circumstances, I wouldn't be so bold, but Miss Thulin has always been like a child of my own, and the professor and I always discussed her as if...well, as if we were her own parents!" She looked back and forth between Sherlock and Imogen. "Was that improper?"

"No, of course not," Imogen assured her. "Not at all."

"Do go on, Mrs. Fletcher," Sherlock urged her.

"So, I asked him what sort of proposal he meant," she continued. "And all he said was, 'Someone with a great deal of influence may wish to buy it. Which would certainly help us all.'"

"Did he elaborate?" Imogen pressed.

"No, ma'am, he was very quiet. Thoughtful," Mrs.

Fletcher said. "But I know he corresponded with this person regularly after that."

"You know who it was?" Watson asked.

She shook her head.

"No, sir, but I recognized the stationery, and the seal— no envelope, just a wax seal. And every time he received one of those letters, he would stay awake late into the night, looking into the fire."

"What did the seal look like?" Sherlock wondered.

"A coat of arms, sir," she replied. "With an eagle, displayed, right in the center. No other symbols. I could never read the motto—it was too small."

"I suppose he burned these letters, after answering them," Sherlock mused.

"I don't know, sir," Mrs. Fletcher admitted. "I never found any pieces of paper in the fire, but that doesn't mean he didn't burn them to ash. But..." Mrs. Fletcher's fingers tightened around themselves, and she went pale.

"Please speak, Mrs. Fletcher," Sherlock said evenly. "If you fear you've done something that may endanger your current position here, I assure you that any help you can provide in this regard far outweighs any indiscretion— especially an indiscretion motivated by concern for Miss Thulin."

"Yes, sir," Mrs. Fletcher said in a rush, looking plaintively at Imogen. "Please don't think that I make a habit of this, Mrs. Fleetwood—I usually wouldn't dare poke through any private papers, but this seemed to me to be an emergency. Miss Thulin had been killed, I thought—but then Mr. Basil Collingwood suddenly arrived at the house in Oxford *with her*, and she couldn't speak, and it became very clear that the professor had lied to all of us for some terrible reason..." She swallowed hard. "Such a darkness had come over him since he'd returned home from that party, and begun corresponding with that stranger, I knew it must be connected. So, I combed through the professor's study...and I found one letter, tucked into a book, on his desk."

"From the professor to this stranger, or from the stranger to the professor?" Sherlock suddenly demanded.

"From the stranger, to the professor," Mrs. Fletcher said.

Sherlock shot to his feet, pinning her with his gaze.

"Do you have it?"

"Erm...Yes, sir, I have it in my things upstairs—"

"Go get it at once," he commanded. "This instant— bring it right back here."

She hesitated—

"Hurry, Mrs. Fletcher, this is very important," Imogen urged her, standing up, too. Mrs. Fletcher bustled quickly out of the room. Sherlock stood where he was for a moment, then turned and began to pace in front of the window, his brow stormy, his eyes dark. He hooked his thumbs in his waistcoat pockets and lowered his head.

"Who could this stranger be?" Watson wondered, glancing at Imogen. "Someone from the continent, in Germany or France?"

"Doubtful, since the professor met him at a party in Oxford," Sherlock muttered. "Certain types of people mix together at such small, academic gatherings—but not usually foreign spies."

"Here it is, sir," Mrs. Fletcher came back, breathless, holding out a piece of paper. Sherlock lunged toward her and took the paper, came back to the window and studied it intently.

"Excellent paper, from here in London," he muttered, turning it over and weighing it in his fingers. He took out a small magnifying glass from his coat pocket, and, tilting the paper toward the light, examined the red seal. Imogen and Watson pressed closer to him, looking over his shoulders.

"The wax is English, too," he observed. "And Mrs. Fletcher has a remarkable eye for heraldry. It is indeed an eagle, displayed. And the motto..." He peered through the glass, while Imogen held her breath.

"It is Irish Gaelic," Sherlock declared. "'From the Sea Comes Justice.'"

"What does the letter say?" Watson prompted. Sherlock swiftly opened it, and read aloud.

"'Sir, I am in receipt of your note. Please allow me until next week to fully respond to your questions. -M.'"

"Just 'M'?" Watson peered at the paper, too. "That doesn't give us much."

"Indeed, Watson, you are mistaken," Sherlock countered. "This is a right-handed gentleman, very well-educated, deliberate and calculating. You can judge him by his purposeful, strident and measured handwriting: he is a chess player in all respects, never a gambler. He uses a fine pen, and black India ink, which indicate that he prefers to deal with people through correspondence rather than in person, and he wants his meaning to come across with absolute clarity. The flourishes around the 'M' suggest that he is intent upon everyone knowing that he is a man of importance, position and power. English is his first language, but I doubt that it is his only language."

Sherlock suddenly turned around, facing them and briskly folding the letter. He addressed Mrs. Fletcher.

"May I keep this?"

"Certainly, sir," Mrs. Fletcher answered. "I have no use for it."

"Thank you." He tucked it into his coat. "Watson and I must dash out to look into something, and we shall be back in time for dinner."

"Of course," Imogen said. Mrs. Fletcher left to fetch the gentlemen's coats and hats. Watson headed toward the door, and Sherlock started that way—

—before he stopped, hesitated, then turned back to face Imogen. He reached down and took up her right hand, looking right at her, that darkness returning to his eyes.

"Now that we have established that there is quite possibly another villain in this case," he said gravely. "And that this villain is more than likely still among the living, I would advise that neither you nor your servants speak of this 'M' person to anyone for the time being. It is possible we have stumbled across a secret that may yet hold some danger."

"Yes, I understand," Imogen said, returning the pressure on his fingers. "We won't mention it outside this house."

"Thank you," Sherlock said, and released her hand. "We'll come back later."

And with that, Sherlock and Watson put on their coats and hats, and swept out of the house, leaving Imogen to ponder everything alone.

Chapter Seven

Tuesday, December 19th

Basil sat in his chair by the fireplace, drumming his fingers rapidly on the armrest. A book lay open and limp in his other hand. He stared straight at the window, its lace curtains drawn. Daylight came in, but he couldn't see the street.

He slapped the book shut, stood up and tossed the book down into his chair. Pressing his hands together under his chin, he started to pace—first toward the fireplace, then away from it, then back to the fireplace again. The floorboards squeaked beneath his every step, but he hardly heard it. He glanced at the clock on the mantle.

Five minutes to eleven. He was usually early...

Basil turned away from the clock and paced toward the bookshelves, scanning the spines without seeing them.

"Sir?"

Basil jumped, and glanced back over his shoulder. Mrs. Butterfield stood in the hall doorway, watching him.

"What is it, Mrs. Butterfield?" he asked impatiently, raking his hand through his hair.

"Would you like some tea, sir?"

"No, thank you," he muttered, reaching down to rearrange a pile of papers on the piano.

"You seem uneasy, sir," she noted carefully.

Basil snorted—then felt a pang of terror shoot through

his heart.

"I suppose I am," he confessed, pushing the papers aside and squeezing the bridge of his nose between his fingers. "I wasn't half this nervous when I asked Victoria to marry me."

"Perhaps it's because you knew the answer."

Basil looked across at his housekeeper, who gave him a bit of a sad smile. Basil swallowed.

"Perhaps you're right," he murmured.

"I'll make some tea," she decided, and headed back toward the kitchen.

Basil took a deep breath, rammed his hands in his pockets, and looked at the clock again. It was eleven, on the dot. He should be here. He should be here right—

Tap, tap, tap!

Basil didn't wait. He crossed the floor with long, swift strides, opened the inner door, hurried through the entryway and opened the front door himself.

Fred Brody stood outside, his hand still suspended from knocking. He wore a smart grey suit, blue tie, and grey top hat. His blue eyes flashed to Basil's, his eyebrows went up— and though he offered a small smile, his face went pale.

Basil stilled. His heart started hammering against his ribs.

"Fred," he said quietly—gently.

"Good morning, Basil," Fred ventured, just as quietly. "I'm sorry, I'm...a bit late."

"Not at all," Basil shook his head, closely studying his friend's features. Fred Brody was exceedingly handsome—

had always been the delight of any young lady in his company, with his dark hair, bright eyes, athletic build and aristocratic features. But what had always made him charming, and what Basil enjoyed most about him, was an inherent sparkle, a cheerful and effervescent optimism that brought sunshine into even the darkest scene.

But now, as Basil looked at him…

That sparkle seemed absent. As if it had faded away beneath a cloud.

"Do come in," Basil urged him quickly. "Come out of the cold!"

"Thank you," Fred answered, taking off his hat and following Basil inside. Basil led the way, but his heart hadn't stopped hammering, and his throat felt tight. As he opened the inner door, he found Mrs. Butterfield waiting there with a ready smile.

"Good morning, Lord Brody!" she said warmly. "Let me take your coat and hat."

"Thank you, Mrs. Butterfield—how are you?" Fred asked, some color coming back to his face as he handed her his effects.

"Splendid, splendid—we're all getting ready for Christmas," she answered as she took them. "The tree should arrive this afternoon."

"I'm sure it will be quite an event this year, with Mr. and Mrs. Collingwood home to enjoy it," Fred observed.

"Oh, indeed," Mrs. Butterfield agreed. "I cannot tell you how excited Miss Imogen is, she's like a schoolgirl."

Fred let out a soft laugh and lowered his head—and Basil felt pain center around his heart. Not for the first time, he wondered if Fred had once been secretly in love with Imogen.

"The tea will be ready in a moment, sirs," Mrs. Butterfield said as she hung up Fred's things, and went back to the kitchen.

"Well, come in, sit down," Basil invited. "Did you...find my Christmas card?"

"Oh—yes, we did," Fred replied, glancing at him as he came in front of the fireplace and seated himself on the couch. "I was astonished."

"I thought I ought to stop being such a misanthrope," Basil said, still standing as he mustered a teasing smile. "It suits a confirmed bachelor, but not a married man."

Fred's head came up, and he looked at Basil in surprise.

"Married?" he repeated. And he lost his color again. "To...Victoria?"

Basil stopped. His smile faded—and now that pain accompanied the rapid pace of his pulse.

"Yes, of course," he said. "Did you...think there might be another lady?"

"Well...there was a long time when I thought that you and Maria would..." Fred stopped, looking up at him. "Which is why I...I thought perhaps that Victoria..." He glanced down, squeezing his fingers together. He gave a brief, crooked smile. "I suppose I did see you together at Heathfell, after it burned. I should have realized that I..." He looked into the fire, his gaze distant. "And then Harold…"

"Fred," Basil said, hardly able to bear it, and sat down in the chair across from him—leaning forward. "Fred, you have been my closest and dearest friend for nearly ten years. In spite of my foul tempers and disinclination to be social in the slightest, you have continuously been kind, friendly, and inclusive to me. And you helped with the Winchester situation more than you could possibly know. You saved my life at Heathfell." His voice quieted. He wished his friend would look at him…

"I am truly sorry for any pain I may have caused you. How I have disregarded you in the past. Taken you for granted," Basil went on quietly. "But I don't intend to do that anymore. Friends such as you can never be bought—and indeed, might never be found again once lost." Basil interlaced his own hands together and squeezed, half-praying… "Fred, would you do me the honor of being the best man at my wedding?"

Fred's head came around. His eyes flashed, and focused on Basil's.

"But…" he said. "Won't Captain Fleetwood be—"

"I haven't asked him," Basil shook his head. "Everyone knows that you are my first choice for that position."

Fred blinked.

"But don't you think that a member of your family ought to—"

"You *are* my family, Fred," Basil insisted. "You always have been. I've just been too foolish to realize it."

Fred looked down, and smiled quietly. Then, he looked up at Basil, still smiling...

But the sorrow behind his expression overwhelmed it all.

"Thank you," he said. "And I...I'm honored. I truly am. But I'm afraid that I can't."

"You can't?" Basil's heart plunged. "Why?"

"I'll not be living in London anymore," Fred said, lightly tapping the armrest. "After Mother died, and now Harold...and Robert is constantly away from home...I'm certain Maria has designs to marry someone-or-other..." He heaved a sigh and covered his eyes. "I can't bear it—I can't bear the nonsense, the parties, the social calls. She's become so entangled with all of it, it's like she's forgotten me entirely." Fred dropped his hand and stared at the rug. "I'm going to an old family cottage in the country, near Newcastle."

"Good lord, that's far away," Basil murmured, his hands growing cold.

Fred nodded.

"That's the intention," he said quietly. "Perhaps I can set myself up as a teacher of reading or Latin, or I could even make a study of the flora and fauna. Live quietly. Keep chickens. Find a lady who enjoys my company, and have a few children." He glanced at Basil. "Something like what you're planning to do, I imagine."

Basil didn't answer. Instead, he rubbed his thumbs together and ventured a question.

"When do you leave?"

"End of March," Fred said. "I would go directly after Christmas, but I'm horrified of the thought of moving all my possessions that far north in the snow and ice." Fred met his glance again. "When do you marry?"

"I believe Victoria's settled on the end of May," Basil murmured. "Would you...consider at least coming to the wedding?"

Fred smiled reflexively again.

"I will give you my new address. Please send me an invitation," he said. "And if I cannot come, I'd be happy to have a piece of the cake."

"You'll be the first on the list," Basil promised.

Fred glanced up at the clock.

"I'm sorry, I ought to go," he said. "I still have some Christmas shopping to do before it snows again." He got to his feet.

Thrown, Basil stood up also.

"Of course—yes, of course, don't let me keep you," Basil stammered. "I'll...I think Mrs. Butterfield is still in the kitchen—"

"It's all right, I can find my own things," Fred assured him. "Don't trouble her." And he stepped around and opened the inner door. Then, he stopped, his hand on the knob, and lowered his head.

Basil held his breath. Fred turned slightly, and looked at him.

"You ought to know...I do not blame you for what

happened to my brother," Fred said quietly. "But he *was* my brother."

"I understand," Basil said, and his voice shook.

Fred paused, as if weighing what more to say.

"Merry Christmas, Basil," Fred finally said.

"Merry Christmas, Fred," Basil answered. And with one last glance, Fred stepped through the door, donned his hat and coat, and left Pendywick Place.

Basil stood where he was, hardly able to breathe, staring at the open door as it slowly swung shut. He set his hands on his hips, his chest hurting.

Footsteps, and wheels, down the hall. Basil turned away.

"Oh!" Mrs. Butterfield cried. "Has he gone already? He wasn't here ten minutes!"

"He had some errands to run, Mrs. Butterfield." Basil moved back to the piano and shifted those same papers.

"I suppose he was honored by your asking him?" she said hopefully.

"He was," Basil murmured. "But he declined."

"Declined? Whatever for?"

"He's..." Basil cleared his throat. "He's moving to Newcastle. At the end of March. He says he's tired of London."

"Oh," Mrs. Butterfield said mournfully. "Oh, that's terrible. I'm so sorry, sir."

"Thank you, Mrs. Butterfield. You may leave the tea here," he said shortly.

"Yes, sir," she murmured, and trailed back to the kitchen. Basil did not turn around. Instead, he shakily swiped at the hot tears running down his cheeks, folded his arms tight, and leaned his forehead against the bookshelf.

Chapter Eight

Victoria had watched Basil all throughout dinner. He was silent, faraway, and ate methodically. Mr. and Mrs. Collingwood noticed his somber mood—they glanced at him a few times—but they apparently knew their son well enough to allow him room to brood. Instead of pressing him, they talked about what they had done with their day, including Victoria in the conversation. She answered and participated, always keeping a corner of her attention on her fiancé. At last, Mr. and Mrs. Collingwood said they were going to retire and do some reading. Mrs. Butterfield and Susan Sowerby cleared away the supper dishes while everyone got to his feet. Basil absently kissed his mother goodnight and wandered out into the hallway, his hands in his trousers pockets.

"You'd better go talk to him, dear," Mrs. Collingwood whispered pointedly to Victoria. "I daresay something's gone wrong, either with one of his patients or his friends."

/ *Oh, dear,*/ Victoria signed, her brow tightening. / *He was going to ask Fred Brody to be his best man in the wedding today—do you think it might have something to do with that?*/

"I hope not," Mrs. Collingwood said earnestly. "I dearly love Fred, and I know Basil does, too. But after that nasty business with his brother..."

Victoria swallowed, feeling cold, and nodded.

"Good luck," Mr. Collingwood winked at her. "We'll see you in the morning."

/*Goodnight,*/ she bid them, and watched them leave the room. Victoria stood thinking for a quiet moment, then gathered herself and ventured out into the dark, chilly hall.

She paused in the doorway, gazing into the parlor. The garlands and tree had arrived that afternoon. The servants had dressed the bannisters with the holly and ivy, and Hemsworth had set the tree exactly where it had been the year before—but it was not yet decorated. That would have to wait until the Captain returned from business, and the Fleetwoods could join them for the event. A shadow passed through Victoria as she stood looking across at it—a dark, misplaced tree set against the bookshelves, as if it didn't wish to be there.

And not far from it, in his armchair, Basil sat staring ahead of him into the fire, not seeing anything, his fingers draped over his lips. The firelight glimmered in his eyes, casting shadows across his grave, carven features and his darkened brow. Jack lay beside him on the rug, paws folded, head resting on them. Listening to the crackle of the hearth.

As quietly as she could—though the floor creaked with every step—Victoria ventured into the room. Without signing anything, since he wasn't looking at her, she drew up in front of Basil, then gathered her skirt and knelt down beside his left knee, facing him. She leaned her right shoulder against the side of the chair, reached across his lap and interlaced her fingers with his.

He drew in a slow breath and returned the pressure on her hand, arranging his grasp so that it fit comfortably with hers.

"Fred came to see me today," he murmured, his deep voice quiet and sonorous. Victoria couldn't say anything, but she wouldn't have if she could. She just waited. Basil raised his eyebrows and glanced down.

"He says he's moving to Newcastle in March. It isn't likely that he'll even be able to attend the wedding."

Watching him, Victoria canted her head in question. He glanced at her for a moment.

"It's Harold," he answered. "And it seems that Maria is refusing to grieve or even face what has happened. Instead, she's cluttering up her life with social engagements and other nonsense. Leaving poor Fred to manage all on his own. And of course, Robert has never been a stay-at-home." He heaved a sigh and rubbed his eyes with his free hand. Victoria just leaned against his leg and gripped his hand with both of hers, stroking the back of it. He looked down at her again, meeting her eyes and considering her face.

"You're fond of Fred, aren't you?"

Victoria nodded quickly. Basil's gaze softened.

"He's fond of you, too," he said. "I do think...if circumstances were different...that he would have come."

Victoria nodded again, setting her chin on his knee. He lowered his left hand and touched her hair, stroking the top of her head. She closed her eyes, treasuring the warm, gentle sensation.

"Did you enjoy shopping with Mother and Imogen today?" he asked. "I'm afraid I wasn't listening to anything during dinner."

"Mhm," Victoria sighed.

"Go to Leadenhall Market?"

"Mhm."

"Buy any presents for me?"

Victoria, her eyes still shut, grinned.

"Hhm-mm," she grunted, shaking her head.

"Right, of course not," he answered. "What was I thinking?"

She giggled and opened her eyes. He was gazing back down at her, wearing a soft smile now, which warmed all his features. She bent her head and kissed his knee.

"Did you meet anyone you knew during this excursion?" he asked.

Victoria gasped, and sat up straight.

"What?" Basil demanded, eyes widening. She pulled her hands free of his.

/ I forgot to tell you—something extraordinary happened,/ she signed quickly. */ We passed a bookstore, and our language was there in the window—a beautiful copy of Thulinian. Imogen and your mother went inside, and I was standing there looking at it—and a gentleman came up to me./*

"A gentleman?" Basil frowned intently. "Who was he?"

/ He introduced himself as Professor X-A-V-I-E-R C-H-U-R-C-H-I-L-L,/ She spelled it out so that Basil clearly

understood. /*He had overheard what we had been talking about, and presumed that I was Professor Thulin. He is a professor of languages at the University of London, and had been meaning to write to me to ask if I would create another language for him!*/

Basil was startled.

"Another language? What for?"

/*He says he's had his students learning Thulinian and they seemed so eager that he wanted to open up the study to the invention of languages, in the modern day,*/ she explained. /*He said he would pay me for my efforts, and be at my disposal if there was ever anything I might need.*/

"Anything you might need?" Basil repeated. "Such as?"

/*The school, Basil,*/ she signed emphatically, getting up on her knees. /*He understood me when I signed to him—I didn't need an interpreter! What if, instead of paying me, we did an exchange? My services in exchange for his? I create a language or more languages for his school, and he could come teach at ours?*/

"My love, you certainly remember what a time of it we had up in Yorkshire," Basil said frankly, looking at her. "And we were simply trying to re-write something that had already been invented. You're speaking of creating something entirely new, the way you did before—only this time, you have very little ability to read or write."

Victoria was already shaking her head.

/*When we were trying to recreate Thulinian, the difficult part was trying to remember exactly what I had done,/* she said. */Because if I deviated—or improved it, as I was sometimes tempted to do—then it wouldn't be the same language, and Winchester might still be able to use the copy he had. This time, I would have total freedom, and the experience of having done it once before—and you and Imogen to help me!/*

"It would still be an enormous endeavor—and endlessly frustrating for you to have things read out to you instead of being able to read them," Basil stated. "Are you willing to go through all that again?"

/Happily,/ Victoria said quickly. */Because I think Professor Rochester is right—England truly needs a school like the one we wish to build. And I don't see how we can achieve what we wish to do with only three professors. If there is something I can do to help, I am going to do it./*

Basil considered her, brow furrowed in thought. At last, he smiled, and touched her cheek with his thumb.

"'Though she be but little,'" he quoted. "'…she is fierce.'"

Victoria turned her head and kissed his fingers.

Basil looked away, as if suddenly captured by a thought, and drummed his fingers on the armrest.

"Professor Xavier Churchill, did you say?"

"Mhm," Victoria agreed.

Basil suddenly got up from the chair, turned and headed to the shelves. Jack instantly hopped up and followed him, eager to help. Victoria, watching Basil curiously, got her feet under her, stood and then sat down on the couch. Basil snatched the thick, black volume of the Social Register off the shelf, spun around and flipped it open. In the next motion, he pulled his spectacles out of his pocket and put them on.

"Professor Xavier Churchill..." he muttered as he turned the pages. "Carteret, Cavendish, Cecil, Chichester, Cholmondeley...Churchill." He sat down on the couch next to her, their shoulders touching. Jack sat attentively in front of them, listening and watching.

"Good lord, there are quite a few of them," Basil commented. "Let's see...Ah, here we are. Xavier Churchill the Second, Professor. He's been teaching language at the University of London for ten years, and before that, at St. Albans for five years, and before that, the Royal Grammar School Worcester for seven years."

/*Goodness, that's...twenty-two years,*/ Victoria frowned.

Basil glanced at her.

"Not expecting that?"

She peered at the book—but of course, she couldn't read it without study, and she was too impatient.

/*When does it say he was born?*/

"Erm...August 9th, 1837."

Victoria hesitated, her gaze unfocusing.

"What?" Basil pressed.

/*That would make him forty-five years old?*/ she looked at him again. He nodded.

"Yes," His eyes narrowed. "Did he not look forty-five?"

Victoria shook her head.

/ *No, he didn't. If I were to make a guess, I would say that he was thirty-five or thirty-six. He was tall and good-looking, even athletic. And he seemed to have just come from a hot, sunny climate.*/

"Hmm," Basil growled, shutting the book and sitting back in the couch. "I've seen young men look a good deal older than they were, due to hard living, or illness, or just the bad London air. But I can't say it's very common for a man to look ten years *younger* than he ought to be." He tapped the cover of the book. Then, he looked at Victoria sideways. "Are you as curious as I am?"

/ *I have to say yes, I am,*/ Victoria agreed. / *How could we find out more about him?*/

"We could walk to the University tomorrow," Basil suggested. "They might have odd hours, though, because of the holiday—but if that fails, we can visit the library. What do you think?"

/ *Yes,*/ Victoria agreed. / *It could be that there's simply a mistake in the register, about his tenure at one of the schools—but I'd like to set it straight, and know for certain who he is.*/

"Mmmmrrrr," Jack growled expectantly, his tail wagging.

"What?" Basil demanded of him.

/ *You said the word,*/ Victoria said, smiling crookedly.

"What, Walk?" Basil raised his eyebrows.

"YIP!" Jack barked, nearly splitting their eardrums.

"Good lord!" Basil cried, wincing away. "Jack, *no.*"

/He hasn't been a walk today,/ Victoria acknowledged sheepishly. */I think we all forgot him./*

"Mrrrrrr," Jack muttered again, shifting his weight. Basil sighed and glanced at the clock.

"Well, we have time for one turn around the block," he said, then looked at Victoria. "Want to join us on a little caper?"

/With pleasure!/

Wednesday, December 20th

Dr. Watson hurried down the street with his friend, trying to keep pace with the taller man, who had picked up his walking stick so as to extend his strides. The streets of London seemed even more clamorous and thickly-crowded than usual, what with the rush of Christmas coming on, and the chill in the air made the steam from various engines and fires roll like clouds down the alleys.

The two men dashed along the sidewalk, across the street—dodging cart and hansom—and lighted on the opposite curb in front of a well-appointed building on Broad Street, with a sign above the door which read: *Boyle, Carter and Blast.*

"This is it, then?" Watson panted, glancing across the façade.

"Indeed, Watson," Holmes leveled a cold look at the

black door. "We may need to prepare for battle."

"Battle, what do you mean?" Watson looked at him sharply.

Holmes turned and regarded him plainly.

"If we are indeed attempting to uncover that which is both nefarious and secret about our late Professor Winchester, there is reason to suspect that his solicitor will not be so eager to divulge it," he said, and lifted an eyebrow. "However, I do not intend to leave here without obtaining what I want." And with that, he strode up to the door and smoothly went inside. Watson followed.

They took off their hats, finding a busy little clerk just inside, writing away at a desk. Holmes swiftly asked him for Mr. Boyle, and the clerk gave them stammered directions to follow the stairs to the second floor, and proceed to the third office. Holmes immediately swept toward the staircase, Watson hurrying after, and in a moment, they had achieved the second story, and found themselves in a long, plain hallway flanked by office doors. Holmes strode to the third door, and pointed to the name upon the plate, giving Watson a pointed look.

"Here's our man, Watson," he murmured, then rapped on the frosted glass.

"Come in?" came a thin voice from inside. Holmes twisted the knob and plunged inside, Watson on his heels. They had entered a small office, flanked on all sides by filing cabinets and shelves, all meticulously clean and organized. Ahead of them stood a wide desk with a lamp and several stacks of paper. A thin, balding man with spectacles and a pinched face sat behind the desk, his pen poised above a piece of paper. His large eyes fixed on them.

"Can I...help you?" he asked.

"Mr. Boyle, forgive us for disturbing you," Holmes said coolly. "I am Sherlock Holmes, and this is my friend and colleague, Dr. Watson."

Mr. Boyle blinked and frowned, then put down his pen.

"How can I be of service to you gentlemen?"

"We have recently learned that you were solicitor to the late Professor Harcourt Winchester, is that correct?" Holmes asked him, stepping closer.

The man's attention sharpened.

"I'm...sorry, I cannot divulge client information."

"Even if that client is dead?" Holmes canted his head, his eyes flashing.

Mr. Boyle swallowed.

"Well, yes," he said, summoning what firmness he could. "Unless you have something from the police..."

"Mr. Boyle, I am a consulting detective," Holmes interrupted. "And I am currently representing a young woman named Victoria Thulin—do you recognize that name?"

"I..." Mr. Boyle stammered—and some color came into his pallid face.

"I see that you do," Holmes concluded. "Were you also aware that, a little more than a year ago, Professor

Winchester brutally attacked this young woman, severing her tongue and leaving her by the side of the road to meet her death?"

Mr. Boyle's mouth sagged open.

"I...sir, no, I hadn't heard—"

"Fortunately, Miss Thulin survived this encounter, and is now my client," Holmes stated. "And therefore, it is my duty that no further mischief befalls her from this quarter. Therefore, I would very much appreciate being able to study Professor Winchester's official documents."

"But...Mr. Holmes..." Mr. Boyle tried. "It's true, Professor Winchester *is* dead! How could he do anything when he's in his grave?"

"That," Holmes leaned down toward him, his voice like a knife edge. "Is precisely what I want to know." He gave Mr. Boyle a dangerous smile. "So, Mr. Boyle, if you would be so kind as to show us all you have on the late professor, we would be obliged to you."

Chapter Nine

Holmes suddenly got up from his chair, causing Watson to jump and glance at his friend. Mr. Boyle had left to take tea in a neighboring room, leaving Holmes and Watson alone in the office, with Winchester's papers spread out before them on the desk. The two men had been pouring over them for nearly an hour now.

"What is it, Holmes?" Watson asked, frowning as he set down an old receipt. Holmes didn't answer right away. Instead, he moved to the window, pressing a forefinger to his lips, and stared absently through the panes and down at the street.

"Did you find something?" Watson pressed.

"Mm," Holmes grunted, then met Watson's eyes for just an instant before returning his attention to the window. "What have *you* found, Watson?"

"Not much of great interest," Watson admitted. "Household bills paid on time, servants' salaries, traveling expenses for lectures..."

"Exactly, Watson," Holmes noted. "Nothing much of interest."

"That is what troubles you," Watson observed. Holmes raised his eyebrows at him.

"Shouldn't it? A man loses everything to debtors, yet

his affairs seem to be perfectly in order?"

"It doesn't smell right, to be sure," Watson agreed. "And...well, doubtlessly you've noticed already..."

"Noticed what?" Sherlock canted his head. "That both the Heathfell Hall and the Bath house are conspicuously missing from these records?"

"That's it exactly," Watson nodded. Holmes swept back toward the desk, frowning at the pile through which he had been searching.

"And there is also *this*." Holmes lifted a brown ledger from beneath several papers, opened it, and turned to a page very near the end of the book. "What do you make of it?" He spun the book around and handed it to Watson.

"What, the last entry?"

Holmes just nodded quickly, bending his arms and hooking his fingers in the pockets of his waistcoat. Watson's brow furrowed as he studied the careful, strident handwriting along the columned lines—Winchester's handwriting, marking out monthly expenses.

"It says here...'Mortgage: 1,000 pounds,' and in the paid column it says, 'In full.'"

"And the memo?" Holmes lifted an eyebrow.

Watson looked at it—then sharply up at his friend.

"It says 'M.'"

"Indeed," Holmes' cold eyes flashed. "Our mysterious Mr. M."

"So—this Mr. M paid the mortgage for him that month?"

"That may be a safe assumption," Holmes allowed. "What is the date, there?"

"Erm...April 5th, 1881," Watson read.

"Just months before his disastrous encounter with Miss Thulin," Holmes murmured, turning away again, his eyes piercing through that which Watson could not see. He stepped slightly past Watson, and rested his fingers on the back of Watson's chair as he continued to ponder. Watson kept studying the ledger.

"Watson, I believe it is also safe to assume that our dear Mr. Boyle, whatever he may think, is not in possession of *all* of Professor Winchester's vital documents," Holmes stated.

"Where are they, then?" Watson demanded. "In a bank vault somewhere?"

Holmes clicked his tongue and shook his head.

"Winchester has gone to great lengths to keep this association with Mr. M a secret," he noted, turning and stepping around the desk, casting his gaze over the papers. "Yet he is a meticulous record-keeper. He would want to keep these particular records away from *any* prying eyes, yet he was astute enough to know he needed to mind these dealings carefully himself." Holmes looked directly at Watson. "He did not trust Mr. M—that much is clear. I doubt he trusted anyone. He almost certainly did not personally know Mr. M, if they ever even met at all, which is cause enough for great caution. But Winchester's dealings with him were certainly not, as they say, 'on the up-and-up,' or he wouldn't have been so frightened of discovery."

"So, you're certain the professor kept records, but not here," Watson realized. "And not in a bank."

"Where would a man usually keep that which is most valuable to him, Watson, if he did not trust a bank?" Holmes prompted.

"Well, *most* valuable, he would keep it on his person," Watson surmised. "But if that wasn't possible, he would keep it in a safe and private place, like his bedroom or his study, where only he had the key."

"Precisely, Watson!" Holmes hissed, his eyes aflame. "His own home, in his own, private haunts."

"I do hope you don't mean Heathfell Hall," Watson exclaimed. "It burnt to the ground!"

"No, not Heathfell," Holmes scoffed, waving it off. "Too far away, out of his reach, his control. A man would bury a treasure in such a place, but he wouldn't keep these documents there—he might need to get his hands on them in a moment's notice."

"His everyday house, then," Watson proposed. "His home in Oxford."

"Very likely, Watson," Holmes nodded gravely, taking the ledger from him. "We must find out." He slapped the ledger shut and tossed it onto the desk, then swooped to pick up his hat, coat and walking stick. Watson scrambled up to gather his own effects, and hurried out of the office just as Mr. Boyle was returning from his tea.

/*I have never been here...*/ Victoria signed as she glanced around in awe, trying to keep her footsteps quiet. Basil smiled a little at her as they paced down a long, silent aisle, hearing only the distant ticking of an old clock.

Victoria and Basil had finished their breakfast and promptly set off from Pendywick Place, taking Jack for a brisk walk around Hyde Park before leaving him at Imogen's house and proceeding to the University of London. They found it was indeed closed to the public for the holiday, to reopen two days after Christmas. So, the two of them had made their way to the library.

Once they had passed through the tall, marbled entryway, the two had ventured into the maze of dark wooden shelves, the scent of old books filling their lungs, as a sense of immense quiet swallowed them.

Victoria had often visited the library at Oxford. Secretly, of course—women were not allowed in. But she had learned of back doors and side passages, and she had been quiet enough to sneak past the librarians and professors, climb up to the "stacks," and lose herself for an entire day in the Iliad, Beowulf, and various translations of the Bible.

The smell in here was the same. The air tingled with magic, just as it had then. The cavernous silence seemed to hold infinite whispers, beckoning this way and that down a myriad of pathways, like a dark, living forest illuminated by will o' wisps...

"I believe it's somewhere this way..." Basil whispered as

they passed row after row of tall shelves on either side of them, until he finally turned her down one narrow aisle and started glancing across the spines of the books. Victoria looked across the volumes too, frowning hard, pausing sometimes to discern individual letters, fighting to piece them together into words...

"Mm. Here," Basil said, reaching up to pull a thick blue volume down from an upper shelf. He caught it in both hands, then turned to the far end and peered that direction. "I see a table that way," he noted, and Victoria followed him until they came to a table built into the shelf, with a chair in front of it. Basil cleared his throat, handing his hat to Victoria as he pulled out the chair and sat down, laying the book out in front of him. Quickly, he took out his spectacles and put them on, then opened the book and started flipping through the pages. Victoria drew near him, watching intently over his shoulder.

"Here we are," Basil noted softly, pointing. "Professor Xavier Churchill. Born in Surrey to Martha and Alexander Churchill; three brothers: Windom, James and Horace; It lists his grandparents and great grandparents, aunts and uncles...Hm. The same school information we read before. Married once, to a Mary de Lacy; widowed five years later. No children. Never married again. No address listed. Member of St. James Garlickhythe church. As of last year, employed at the University of London..." Carefully, Basil turned a page. "And there he is." He pointed to a photograph. "Is that your man?"

Victoria almost dropped the hat. She grabbed Basil's shoulder and leaned over him, staring at the picture. And before she knew it, she was shaking her head.

"No?" Basil exclaimed, a little too loudly. She looked right at him, and shook her head harder.

"It *isn't* him?" Basil clarified. Victoria quickly set the hat down to free her hands.

/ *This isn't the same man at all!!* / she insisted. / *This man is old—look at him! He has a white beard, no hair! The man I met was young and handsome, and tanned, with just a mustache. This is not the same man at all.* /

"You were right to be suspicious about his age," Basil growled. "Something else is afoot, here."

/ *Who was it who spoke to me, then?* / Victoria pressed. / *Why would he pretend to be this professor? And why would he want me to make another language?* /

Basil considered her, then frowned down at the page.

"I don't know," he admitted. "But perhaps the *real* Professor Churchill could help us."

/ *How can we find him?* / Victoria wondered.

Basil sat back, tapping the page with his finger.

"Why don't we try his church?" Basil suggested. "No doubt they'll know *something* about him."

And with that, the two of them hurried out of the maze of shelves, out of the library—Victoria a great deal more disturbed than she had been when they arrived.

Chapter Ten

"Unfortunately for us," Basil mused as he hopped out of the hansom cab, and helped Victoria down into the icy street. "That card our mysterious professor gave you only has a post office box, not a home address."

Victoria couldn't answer, since Basil held her hand—but she was grateful for his support. They stood in a very narrow street called Little Trinity Lane, which, due to the recent snowstorms and thaws, had turned into a messy, slippery sluice. She shivered against the damp cold as Basil paid the cab driver, then came to stand beside her on the small triangle of paving in front of St. James Garlickhythe.

The bulk of the little church looked to be made of old, pale stone, with tall, arched windows that held hundreds of little square panes. The bell tower, in the center fore, appeared to be a newer addition, all of solid stone, with a hanging black clock and pointed steeple. She took Basil's arm, and together they strode through the black iron gate.

A little carven face peered inquisitively down at them from the Romanesque lintel of the door, as if wondering what business brought parishioners at this time of day. Basil reached out and worked the brass handle, and led Victoria through the door.

A deep hush fell over them. The tap of their steps and the whisper of their clothing echoed softly as they entered the tall, pale room. Simple, Georgian architecture, with strong supporting pillars, plain wooden pews, and an inlaid wooden floor. But large stones also laid into the floor—and Victoria realized that they were probably graves. She couldn't pause long enough to read them, however, so she respectfully stepped around them.

A silvery chandelier hung from the ceiling, burning brightly, and beyond that, the chancel opened up for a lovely wooden altar piece, capped by a dramatic, Renaissance-style painting that appeared to depict the ascension of Christ. Light poured in through all the windows, despite the cloudy day, and Victoria slowed her steps, releasing Basil, drinking in the somber, peaceful quiet—away from the clamor and bustle of the chaotic London streets. Her gaze lingered on the gorgeous painting.

"May I help you?"

Victoria brought her attention down from the heavens to see a thin, pale-haired, carefully-smiling vicar, dressed in black, come out from behind the choir area. He took off his spectacles and came up to them.

"Good afternoon, Vicar," Basil greeted him, holding out his hand. "I'm Basil Collingwood, and this is my fiancée, Victoria Thulin."

"Ah." The vicar's smile warmed as he glanced between the two of them. "You wish to be married?"

Victoria laughed, and Basil shot her a smile.

"Yes, of course—but we are planning the wedding for May—" Basil began.

"Certainly, certainly," the vicar nodded. "Plenty of time to prepare. We do need time for the bans to be read, as you know, and we would like you to attend here regularly before—"

"Forgive me, Vicar, but I'm afraid we're here on another errand entirely," Basil interrupted.

"Oh!" the vicar blinked. "I'm so sorry—how presumptuous of me."

"No, it's no trouble at all," Basil assured him, holding up a hand, then looking at Victoria. "We were wondering if you could help us find someone—a member of your congregation."

"Indeed?" the vicar frowned earnestly. "I will certainly try to help, if I can."

"Do you know a gentleman by the name of Professor Xavier Churchill?" Basil asked, watching him carefully.

The vicar's eyebrows went up—and a change came over his face.

"Oh—yes, indeed. I had the honor of knowing that very kind, goodly gentleman for nearly fifteen years."

Basil and Victoria exchanged a glance.

"He's left here, then?" Basil's brow furrowed. "Could you perhaps tell us where he's gone?"

The vicar smiled gently.

"Of course I can," he nodded. "But I'm afraid that where he's gone, you cannot follow."

Victoria's mouth opened.

"You mean..." Basil said slowly. "He's died?"

"He has, Mr. Collingwood," the vicar nodded sadly. "Not three weeks ago. We performed his funeral in this very church. I've never seen so many people attend a funeral—his present and former students packed the church, standing in the aisles, up in the chancel, everywhere. And even more attended the graveside service."

"How did he die?" Basil asked keenly.

The vicar's face clouded.

"Terrible business. Horribly unfortunate," the vicar said softly. "He cut himself shaving, just here, on his throat." The vicar pointed near his jaw. "It became infected, poisoned his blood. He died in the heat of a fever." The vicar's attention sharpened as he considered the two of them. "I'm sorry you had to find out about him this way—I can see you are distressed."

"Confused, rather," Basil muttered. "Just the other day, Miss Thulin was approached by a man claiming to be Professor Xavier Churchill—he gave her his card." Basil pulled it out of his coat and handed it to the vicar. Startled, the vicar took it, put his glasses back on and stared at it.

"Good heavens..." He looked back up at them in alarm. "Someone...Someone is actually walking around London, masquerading as my old friend?"

"Apparently so," Basil said gravely. "Do you have any idea who that might be?"

"None at all, sir!" the vicar cried, his face turning red. "This...this is outrageous! I...Well, I ought to call the police!"

"We…might do that ourselves," Basil put his hand out and tapped the end of a pew.

"What did this villain want with you?" the vicar wanted to know.

"My fiancée is a very famous language expert," Basil answered. "He said he wanted her to do some work for him, for his curriculum."

The vicar's mouth tightened.

"Very suspicious indeed."

"More suspicious all the time," Basil murmured, gazing at Victoria.

/ And he's left us at a dead end,/ Victoria signed. / He has no address, the university is closed, and the real professor is dead./

"I beg your pardon, I couldn't follow that," the vicar apologized.

"She said we have no more information at all about whoever spoke to her," Basil said flatly, heaving a sigh and glancing around the church. "We have no more leads to follow."

"Well…" the vicar ventured. "If I hear any more about a gentleman trying to impersonate my late friend, shall I contact you?"

"Would you?" Basil said eagerly. "That could be very helpful."

"Of course," the vicar agreed, and took Basil's calling card. After bidding them goodbye, the vicar retreated to wherever he had been studying, and Victoria and Basil turned to leave.

They paused in the aisle for a moment, rather listlessly admiring the large, beautiful organ up in the loft, before trailing out of the church, stymied and frustrated.

"I hope no one sees us skulking around in here."

"Then stay away from the windows, Watson."

Watson winced as he followed the murmur of his furtive friend through the darkened back corridor of the vast, abandoned stone house.

He and Holmes had taken a train to Oxford immediately, and, once they had arrived had walked through the dreamy, misty town until they came to the former residence of Professor Harcourt Winchester. Making certain that no one saw them, they had slipped down a back alley, picked the lock of a servant's door, and effectively broken into the house.

Now, Sherlock Holmes, with a catlike tread, crept swiftly through the house, keen gaze darting back and forth, taking in every detail. Watson followed as best he could, grimacing every time he trod up on a creaky board.

"They're to be auctioning off everything soon," Holmes whispered. "See? All the furniture and paintings are marked with paper numbers."

"Yes, I see," Watson answered, following him down a

corridor and into a large front sitting room to the right, where a tiger skin lay on the floor. Portraits of masters of literature hung on the dark walls, and all manner of exotic trinkets crowded the mantlepiece, indicating that the man who lived here had traveled all over the world. An intimidating bear head hung over the fireplace, snarling silently down at all who entered.

Holmes paused in the center of this room, mid-stride, like a hound on point. He hardly breathed. Watson halted on the threshold, not wishing to disrupt his friend's train of thought.

In a dancerly move, Holmes turned about, head down, brow sharply-furrowed. He lifted a hand, holding up a finger.

"What we are looking for," he began slowly. "...would not be in any ordinary place. Not even in so secure a spot as a safe or a locked drawer. These things he wished to hide from *every* possibility that they might be seen."

"A secret hiding place, then," Watson guessed. "A hidden closet or drawer."

Holmes' eyes flashed to him. He nodded once.

"Yes," he said faintly. He glanced around. "Something that doesn't seem to fit..."

Holmes swept toward the left-hand wall, running his hands fleetly over the wallpaper, the windowsills, the mop board. He made his way toward the corner, meticulous and quick, sometimes stretching high, other times going down on all fours. At last, he came to the side of the mantle, cast a glance across it—

Froze, his hand suspended.

"Watson," he growled.

"What is it?" Watson asked, daring to step closer and come up beside him.

"See something amiss?" Holmes asked.

Watson almost said no—but he stopped himself, took a breath, and forced himself to look closer.

Then, he saw it.

"That...little wooden Chinaman," Watson pointed. "He looks strangely... *worn*, don't you think?"

"Indeed he does, especially compared to his compatriots," Holmes said. "Could it be that he isn't merely a piece of decoration?" And he reached up, grasped the tiny Chinaman—and twisted him.

The figurine turned like a knob—and just beneath him, in the side of the mantle, a drawer popped out.

"By Jove," Watson gasped.

"Here we have it, Watson," Holmes breathed, his eyes blazing. Carefully, he pulled on the drawer, exposing a short, neat stack of papers.

"What are they?" Watson drew closer, looking over Holmes' shoulder.

"They appear to be letters," Holmes said, taking them back toward the window. "Written in a strange script...Some ancient language I don't recognize. I daresay Mycroft could make something of it. And..." Holmes gave Watson a pointed look. "Signed by our dear Mr. M."

"Really!" Watson breathed, following him to look at the letters himself. "It almost looks like Hindi," he remarked.

"Yes, almost," Holmes mused, looking through all of them, one by one. "Fine paper, though. From London. It is safe to assume that these did not come from abroad, no matter the exotic-looking script. And..." Holmes suddenly trailed off as he came to the last letter. His eyes darted wildly over the writing. "This one is in English. 'My dear Professor Winchester. It was such an honor to meet you last evening. I do wish to continue our discussion. Shall we meet for tea tomorrow afternoon, at my house—two o'clock? I remain your humble servant, Prof. R. Moriarty.'"

Chapter Eleven

"Well, my dear, it seems that we've come to an impasse," Basil sighed as he took off his hat and coat, and hung them in the entryway of Pendywick Place. Victoria did the same, frowning to herself. The two pushed through the door, followed by Jack—whom they'd retrieved from Imogen's—and stepped into the parlor. Jack trotted past them down the hallway to the kitchen, to drink out of the pan beneath the ice box. Mrs. Butterfield, who stood on the second landing dusting the portraits, turned to see them enter.

"Well, good afternoon! Did you have any luck?" she asked eagerly.

"Some," Basil answered, running his hand through his hair. "But not the sort of luck we'd like."

"What does he mean?" Mrs. Butterfield asked Victoria.

/He means that we did find the professor,/ Victoria explained. */He has been dead for three weeks./*

"Good heavens!" Mrs. Butterfield breathed, looking at her sharply. "Then...who was it who approached you at the market?"

"We have no idea," Basil said frankly, sighing as he sat down in the chair. "His card refers to a post office box, and we have no clues as to his real name or identity—or what he truly wanted with Victoria."

"That is the part about all of this that troubles me, sir," Mrs. Butterfield admitted, gripping the feather duster. "After what happened to her before…"

Basil looked up at her gravely.

"You've no need to be afraid for Victoria," he said, his tone low and dangerous. "Not this time."

"I hope not, sir," Mrs. Butterfield tapped the handle of the duster in her palm, then turned and started up the stairs. Victoria, standing by the mantle, folded her arms. Basil considered her.

"What is it?"

She didn't answer for a moment—just let her thoughts settle as the warmth from the fireplace soaked into her skirts. Then, she faced him and lifted her hands.

/I think I should write back to him,/ she said.

Basil sat forward, raising his eyebrows.

"You do?"

She nodded.

/He will probably reply,/ she told him. /And we might learn more about him, based on the paper, his handwriting, and anything he mentions./

Basil watched her a moment, and a slow smile lit his features.

"I believe Sherlock Holmes is beginning to rub off on you."

Victoria grinned.

"Very well—you can dictate to me," Basil said, hopping up and going to his desk, sitting down and pulling out a piece of stationery and a fountain pen. He cleared his throat and looked at her. Victoria crossed the room and stood in front of his desk, thinking as she formed her words.

/Dear Professor Churchill; My fiancé is taking dictation for me, for the sake of expediency. I would like to thank you very much for your kind offer. I am still deeply flattered by it. Unfortunately, I am now in the midst of a project that requires all my attention, and doubtlessly will for several months. However, I am eager to learn more about your ambitions for your class, and would be happy to help you with any other matter. Kind regards./

Basil, who had watched her sign each sentence before writing it down, finished out the last phrase, then turned the paper and handed her the pen.

"Here, you can sign it, so he knows it comes from you," he said. Victoria nodded, put her pen down, and swiftly wrote her signature. This, more than any other writing, was very easy. Muscle memory, after all.

Basil took up the letter and blew on the ink, then folded it and put it in an envelope. He then drew out the false professor's card and addressed the envelope, found a stamp in his drawer and affixed it, then took it out the door to the post box. As he went, Victoria came back to the parlor and sat down on the couch, still thinking. Jack, happily panting, came trundling back in and sat down next to her, and she petted his soft coat.

Jack stopped panting and closed his mouth. His ears perked up and he looked at the window.

"Hm?" Victoria wondered.

Jack turned his head sharply toward the door.

Voices outside. Male voices.

The next moment, Basil came back in through the door, leading Sherlock Holmes and John Watson. Jack wagged his tail, got up and went straight to Doctor Watson, who immediately tousled his ears.

/ *Hello!*/ Victoria greeted them with a broad smile. / *How are you gentlemen?*/

However, neither man returned her smile, and Holmes appeared slightly pale.

"We've come to you with a mystery, Miss Thulin," Holmes replied smoothly. "One that I do not have the skill to solve. But I am hoping my cousin can."

"Really?" Basil looked at him intently. "What is it?"

"Do you recognize this language?" Holmes asked, reaching in his coat and taking out several letters. Basil took them and unfolded them, putting on his spectacles as he did.

"Hm!" he grunted suddenly. "Interesting..."

"What is it?" Watson wanted to know.

Basil crossed to the front window and held the letters to the light.

"This is Sanskrit," he replied, his voice deep and intent as he studied the papers closely. "It is an ancient Indian language. Most works of Hindu philosophy were written in this language, and it was used by the royalty and upper classes."

"I knew it looked familiar—like Hindi!" Watson noted.

"Yes, quite," Basil glanced at him before looking back down at the letters. "What *are* these?"

"Can you read them, Basil?" Holmes asked, his grey gaze fixed on Basil.

Basil winced, tilting his head.

"Mmm, somewhat," he confessed. "I'll have to get out my dictionary. It's been a long time since I've studied it."

"Can you get any gist?" Watson wondered.

"Erm…" Basil scanned the letters. "I see the words 'friend,' 'studies,' erm…something like 'endeavor' or 'project;' 'payment,' 'debt,' 'agreement'… 'girl'…'" Basil frowned. "This is the word for 'tongue' or 'language.' And 'new.' New language." Basil suddenly looked up at the two men. He slowly lifted the papers. "Where did you get these?"

Holmes, not taking his eyes from Basil, took a new paper from his other pocket, unfolded it and held it up. Slowly, deliberately, he read it aloud.

"'*My dear Professor Winchester. It was such an honor to meet you last evening. I do wish to continue our discussion. Shall we meet for tea tomorrow afternoon, at my house—two o'clock? I remain your humble servant, Prof. R. Moriarty.*'"

/ *Winchester!*/ Victoria clapped. / *These are* his *papers?*/

"I'm afraid they are," Holmes answered her. "Watson and I took the liberty of visiting his old home in Oxford, which is scheduled to be sold at auction. We discovered a secret compartment in his mantlepiece that contained these letters." Holmes pointed at them. "As you can see, it appears our professor was dealing with someone named Moriarty."

/*Who is that?*/ Victoria demanded, signing fast. Both men shook their heads.

"We don't know," Watson said. "We think it's an Irish surname, but there are Irishmen all over the world. And it might be an alias, at that."

"Obviously, this Moriarty is someone very learned, and very secretive," Holmes deduced. "Why else would he conduct his correspondence in an ancient Indian tongue? In addition, he must have, at one time, moved in close circles with Professor Winchester, to have encountered him by chance somewhere and then asking that Winchester come visit him the very next day for tea—they could not have lived far apart. Most likely, they lived in the same town."

/*Oxford?*/ Victoria realized. /*You think this Moriarty lives in Oxford?*/

"He may have done, at the time," Holmes said. "There's no real way of knowing where he is now."

As they spoke, Basil had moved to the bookshelf and taken down a thick volume, then seated himself at his desk. He took out a piece of paper and began flipping through the book, comparing it to what he saw on the first letter. Then, he began writing down his translation on a fresh sheet of paper.

"Should we leave him alone?" Watson wondered, eying him.

/*It won't take him long,*/ Victoria assured them. /*I'll*

have Mrs. Butterfield bring tea./

Mrs. Butterfield had already been preparing tea for Basil and Victoria, so she simply added a few more tarts and sandwiches, and two more cups, for Holmes and Watson. Doctor Watson gladly sat with Victoria and drank and ate and talked, but Basil let his cup go cold beside him, and Holmes had declined altogether, opting instead to pace in front of the window.

Basil worked rapidly, his pen scraping the paper, his long hands darting, his eyes quick. Then, within an hour, he slammed the book shut, swiped up the translations and came back toward the fireplace.

"Good lord, that was fast!" Watson exclaimed.

Holmes froze where he stood, all attention.

"Here's what they say," Basil said, adjusting his spectacles. *"'Friend, is the new language complete? I seem to recall that, yesterday, you mentioned something about the girl still working at it, in between her heavier studies. I would urge you to encourage her to finish this project in a timely manner, at least before November. I have pressing need for it—and it would be even better to discuss our further dealings in that language, rather than this one, because this one is certainly known, if obscure. Write back to me as soon as possible, and burn this note. -M.'"*

Victoria's blood ran cold. Watson slowly lowered his teacup into his lap.

Holmes took one step, and lighted like a silent thunderhead right behind Victoria's chair. Basil went on.

"*'Friend, Thank you for the sample you sent me. It is a beautiful tongue, isn't it? I have no doubt that those in my organization will have no trouble learning it and putting it into regular use. We may now discuss the subject of payment. You mentioned one or two bills that have been troubling you. What are they, and in what amount? If you please, burn this note. -M.'*"

Basil shuffled the papers carefully. Victoria couldn't move. She felt Holmes rest his hand on her shoulder.

"*'Friend,'*" Basil read on. "*'You are, unfortunately, a man who is living outside his means. I do not need to tell you how unwise that is. However, in this circumstance, I am happy to help you. We cannot have you and our young prodigy turned out into the street, can we? Therefore, I will be transferring 3,000 pounds into your bank account. It should be there within the next three days. This will be deducted from the amount that I will owe you, in future, for the complete language. If you please, burn this note. – M.'*" And at last, Basil reached the last one. "*'Friend, My need for this code grows more pressing every day. Your second deadline approaches, and I am losing patience. I will not send you the rest of the payment until I have that code in my hands, no matter how your creditors howl. But the instant that I do have it, you can rest assured that the money will appear in your account, untraceable, and you will be free to settle your debts. I look for your affirmative word within the week. Burn this note. – M.'*"

"Winchester did not burn the note," Watson observed

gravely.

"No, he did not," Holmes mused, withdrawing his hand from Victoria, and pressing his forefinger to his lips. "That tells us a great deal about him."

"Nothing that I didn't already know," Basil said, blackly tossing the papers into an empty chair. He crossed his arms. "Winchester, for all his cultivation and good manners, wasn't a man to be ordered around. And he would never destroy correspondence in a business transaction, especially if it contained agreements that he would later want proof of."

"It also tells us that, perhaps, he believed he was dealing with someone on the same level as himself," Holmes noted, lifting an eyebrow. "An equal, a peer."

"You don't think he was?" Watson wondered.

"No, Watson," Holmes shook his head, his gaze cold. "I do not."

Chapter Twelve

December 24th

Victoria, on Basil's arm, stepped out of the church door into the night. Snow fell lightly, covering the churchyard in a fresh, white blanket. The snowflakes sparkled in clouds around the lampposts, and made all the headstones glitter. Around some corner, she heard jingling bells on the harness of a carriage horse, doubtlessly conveying some cheerful group to a neighbor's party.

She glanced up at Basil as he shook hands with the parson. Basil wore his sharp black suit and top hat, with a festive scarlet tie. And he was smiling.

She had watched him all through the service as they sat with his mother, his father, his sister, and his brother-in-law, all in a row in one pew. Basil had sat erect and proud as all the people of the congregation, in turns, turned and twisted to see all of the Collingwood family together in church on Christmas Eve for the first time in twenty years. When they stood to sing "Adeste Fideles," he loudly (and quite prettily) sang harmony with Imogen—who delightedly hooked her arm through his and sang at the top of her lungs.

After, the family had been swarmed by old friends eager to shake their hands and ask where in the world they had been. Basil eagerly introduced Captain Fleetwood to anyone who didn't know him, and helped tell the story of Imogen and the Captain's wedding. Victoria couldn't stop grinning all the while. Basil's eyes sparkled like she'd never seen them, and at times he seemed almost boyish.

Now, as all the congregants spilled out of the church, talking noisily, the family gathered on the front walk and looked round at the snow.

"What a beautiful night," Mr. Collingwood sighed. "What a perfect Christmas Eve."

"Yes, indeed," Mrs. Collingwood nodded. "Let's go see David."

Basil's head came around.

"What?"

"Let's go see David," she repeated, and without waiting for them, she started down the path. The others glanced at each other, startled, but Mr. Collingwood only watched his wife. Then, after a moment, he followed her.

Imogen started to cry. Her brow twisted, tears rolled down her cheeks, and she picked up her skirts.

"Wait for me, Mumma!" she called, hurrying after them. The Captain glanced at Victoria and Basil, and smiled. He said nothing, but put on his own top hat and followed his wife.

Victoria looked up at Basil. He was gazing after his family, his eyebrows drawn together, his jaw tight. Victoria reached up and patted his chest.

He let out a short, watery laugh, his breath a fog around his face, lowered his head and pressed his gloved fingers to his eyes. Then, he sniffed, raised his chin and gave her a smile.

"Shall we?"

She nodded quickly, and together they traced the family's footsteps through the graveyard. It was quite dark, and Victoria wondered if they may have gotten lost…

Only to see that Mrs. Collingwood had led them right to the very spot. Mr. and Mrs. Collingwood, Imogen and the Captain all stood in front of David's headstone, arm in arm, looking at it with a sense of wonderment. Then, Victoria and Basil stepped into the row, and saw what they were looking at.

An exquisite holly and pine wreath, adorned with red ribbons and trailing strands of ivy, stood on a stand beside David's grave. It hadn't been there long—the snow had barely touched it. The holly leaves glittered even in the low light.

"How gorgeous!" Mrs. Collingwood sniffed, dabbing at her eyes with a handkerchief. "Who put this here for my baby?"

Basil stepped up and examined it.

"There's no card," he said. "But it is very beautiful."

"What a thoughtful gesture," Mr. Collingwood murmured.

"It's lovely," Imogen managed, swiping away her own tears. "And it'll last all the twelve days of Christmas, looking just like that."

"And here *you* are, Basil," the Captain noted, smiling with a little playfulness as he pointed at the adjoining plot. "How do you feel to be walking about among the living?"

They all chuckled—an unsteady, relieved sound of release.

"Yes...My *dear* boys..." Mrs. Collingwood said, stepping round and wrapping her arm around Basil's. "My dear, sweet boys. And my girl!" She threw her arm around Imogen's shoulder. Imogen collapsed against her mother, pressing her face into her neck.

"How truly blessed I am!" Mrs. Collingwood declared, lifting her eyes to the heavens. "To have such a family, and such a home." And she leaned up and kissed Basil's cheek, kissed Imogen's head, and her husband's lips.

"While you are giving kisses..." the Captain reminded her.

"Oh, come here, that's a good lad!" Mrs. Collingwood took his face in her hands and kissed both his cheeks, then unexpectedly turned on Victoria and wrapped her up in a tight hug.

Victoria's heart jolted. Tears sprang to her eyes. Slowly, she wrapped her arms around Mrs. Collingwood, and set her chin on her shoulder...

Suddenly overwhelmed by the feeling, the scent, of a *mother.*

Something she never knew she had forgotten. But she remembered now.

Victoria shut her eyes and let her tears fall.

"All right then, let's not stand here in the snow blubbering!" Mrs. Collingwood abruptly declared, stepping back and dashing her own tears away. "We have a Christmas dinner to eat!"

And together, arm in arm, the Collingwood and Fleetwood families, and Victoria, left the church and walked home to Pendywick Place, loudly singing carols all the way. Victoria hummed along, sometimes walking with Basil, and sometimes arm-in-arm with Imogen.

When at last they reached Pendywick Place, they were greeted by the delicious scent of turkey and Christmas pudding—and of course, Jack dancing around their feet, and their happy servants taking their coats and hats and ushering them into the dining room. This year, the Collingwoods planned on having two feasts: one on Christmas Eve, and one on Christmas Day—to make up for lost time. And so, they sat down together, they prayed, and they ate. And this year, Mr. Collingwood sat at the head of the table and carved the turkey, which, Victoria could see, gave Basil such an aching sense of delight that he could hardly hide his emotion.

They talked loudly, sometimes over each other, and laughed far too much. They drank wassail and wine, and warmed themselves down to the bones.

After, they took their plates of Christmas pudding out to the parlor, and basked in the glow of the glittering Christmas tree. Victoria, Imogen and Mrs. Collingwood had decorated it with an old box of ornaments they had found hidden in the attic—only Mrs. Collingwood had known where it was. They'd also covered the tree with baubles that they'd obtained on their travels, like masks from Venice, ribbons and figurines from Spain, and little wooden toys from Switzerland and Germany. Each piece had a story, and as they sat with Jack at their feet, and Queenie in Imogen's lap, the Collingwoods regaled them with travel adventures. In turn, Captain Fleetwood told them of his own Christmases in Cornwall with his younger brother, Phillip, who would be coming to visit them tomorrow.

When they'd all finished their pudding, they portioned out half of the presents to be opened now. The others would wait until tomorrow. Victoria received more than she'd ever received at any Christmas in her life. Several pieces of jewelry from Mrs. Collingwood; a scarf, scented soaps, and white gloves from Imogen and the Captain; a Russian nesting doll from Mr. Collingwood; and a beautiful porcelain doll dressed all in white lace from Basil.

"To replace the Christmas doll you lost at Heathfell," he murmured to her as he sat next to her on the couch—and she kissed his cheek.

/ *What shall I name her?*/ she asked.

"What name do you like?"

Victoria considered for a little bit.

/ *I'll call her Noel,*/ she decided. / *So that I'll always remember today.*/

And Basil kissed her in return, on the forehead.

They left the wrappings all over the floor. Queenie soon abandoned Imogen to practice pouncing on the rustling papers, with Jack watching curiously. Victoria went to the piano and began playing carols, and the family circled all around her to sing in three-part harmony—very well. Often, Victoria closed her eyes and played by feel, letting the voices of the people she had come to love wash down over her like liquid light. They sang and sang, every carol they could remember. When they ran out, they came back to the parlor and played Simile and The Minister's Cat until the clock struck midnight.

"Merry Christmas!" Mr. Collingwood declared, lifting his glass of wassail. They all toasted the same.

"We had better be off to bed," the Captain warned. "Or Father Christmas will skip this house."

"We can't have that!" Imogen gasped—and giggled at her husband.

"Sir?"

They all looked to see Mrs. Butterfield in the doorway.

"Yes, what is it?" Basil asked.

"Forgive me, sir, but this was brought by a courier earlier today," Mrs. Butterfield ventured in, holding out a beautifully decorated envelope. "I'm so foolish—I put it in my apron and forgot it, what with all the to-do with Christmas."

"It's all right, Mrs. Butterfield," Basil said, taking it from her and putting on his spectacles.

"Who is it from?" Imogen asked.

Basil took a knife from his pocket and slit open the envelope, then drew out a magnificent Christmas card, ornamented with gold-inlaid angels.

/*How lovely!*/ Victoria exclaimed.

"We ought to keep it and put it on the tree," Mrs. Collingwood decided. Basil opened it, his brow furrowing, then read it aloud.

"'Dear Collingwood Family, I bid you the fondest and brightest greetings of the season. I wanted to let you know that I took the liberty of setting a wreath at your son and brother David's grave today. I recently learned that he died as a child, on this very night, and such a thing grieved me so that I had to express my sympathy, and also my deep respect for you. If you wish, you may leave it to adorn his grave, or you may of course take it home to adorn your door—whatever you do with it will give me great pleasure and honor. I look forward to receiving your entire family at my home very soon. Merry Christmas! -Professor George Rochester.'"

"Really!" Imogen exclaimed. "He was the last person I was expecting!"

"Who were you expecting?" Basil wondered.

"Well, Sherlock Holmes," she confessed. "It would be like him to do something so mysterious, yet so good and honest."

Basil smiled at her.

"Yes, it would. But the wreath was also forward—which is more like Rochester than like Sherlock, I think."

"I believe I like this professor," Mrs. Collingwood decided. "And we must have *him* to dinner, since he has already hosted you once."

They all decided that they should extend an invitation

to him within a few days after Christmas, after receiving such a kind gesture. Then, the matter passed, and they finished their drinks. Mr. and Mrs. Collingwood were the first to retire, followed soon by the captain and a dreamy Imogen.

For several minutes, Victoria and Basil sat alone in the parlor, listening to Mrs. Butterfield and the other servants cleaning up in the kitchen and humming to themselves. At last, Victoria stretched her legs out in front of her and yawned.

/I ought to go to bed./

"Yes—I have no doubt Imogen will get us up early to pretend that Santa Claus has come," Basil muttered. "But...for once, I've outsmarted her."

Victoria looked at him, canting her head.

He grinned.

"*I* am Father Christmas."

/ What do you mean, you are Father Christmas?/ Victoria asked—fully aware that if she had a voice, she would be whispering.

"That's all I'm going to say on the matter," he said, aloof. "Just know that, in the morning, there may be a few more...things...here by the tree than there are now."

Victoria stared at him—and a slow smile spread over her face.

He returned it, his eyes bright in the firelight.

And she leaned up and kissed him. She wrapped her arms around his neck and let her eyes drift shut as their mouths met and mingled. Basil slipped his arms around her and pulled him into his chest. For a long while, they exchanged slow, gentle kisses, not needing to say anything. At last, their mouths parted, and they only gazed softly at each other.

"I love you," Basil said, his voice low as he looked into her eyes.

Victoria smiled, and nodded, stroking his hair by his temple. She gave him one last kiss, then got up from the couch and wrapped her new doll up in her arms. She started toward the stairs, then turned and faced him.

/*Thank you,*/ she said, lifting her head.

/*You're welcome,*/ he signed back. /*Goodnight.*/

She beamed. And with light feet and heart, she ascended the stairs to her tower—wondering how she would *ever* sleep, knowing that another day just as magical as this one awaited her in the morning.

To be continued in...
BOOK TWO:
THE MUTE OF ANTHONY COLLEGE
AND THE NEWSPAPER SCANDAL

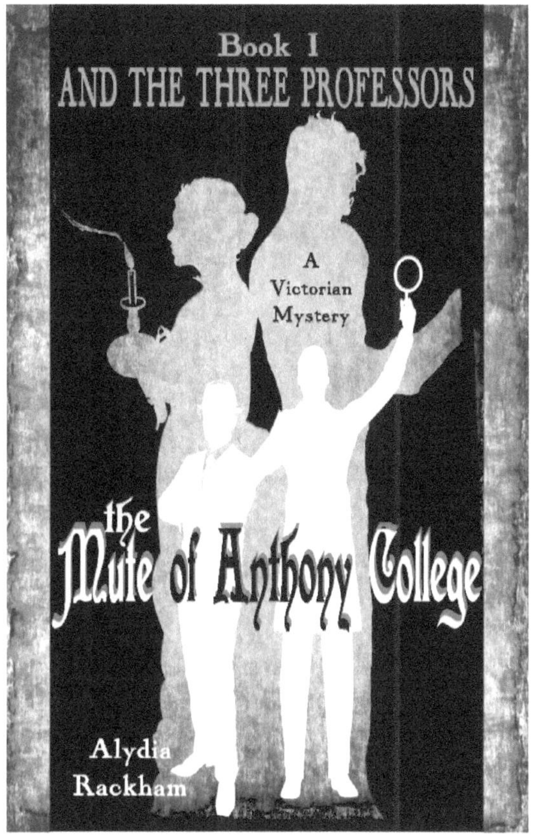

Visit Alydia Rackham's website to get free books, and discover 30+ more fantastic titles!
https://captainrackham.wixsite.com/alydiarackham

THE THREE PROFESSORS

ABOUT THE AUTHOR

Alydia Rackham graduated from McPherson College with a bachelor's degree in English. She has published 75 fanfiction stories and 28 original novels. In addition, she is a singer (winning superior ratings at state competitions in both high school and college), an artist, an avid traveler, and has performed in 20 theatrical productions, 6 short films and one feature-length film to date (winning a Jester Award in high school for the role of Mrs. Higgins in "My Fair Lady," and a gala award for Best Female Performer in a Musical for her role as Mary Poppins in Salina Community Theatre's Production of "Mary Poppins.") She wrote the screenplay for the feature-film "Inkfinger," which was featured in four film festivals, including the Hollywood Dreamz International Film Festival and Writers Celebration in Las Vegas, Nevada, where it was nominated for Best Cinematography. It also won the Award of Merit at the IndieFest Film Awards in La Jolla, California.

SUPPORT ALYDIA RACKHAM ON PATREON!

www.ingramcontent.com/pod-product-compliance
Lightning Source LLC
Chambersburg PA
CBHW020525160726
47992CB00005BA/2258